Off Track

Off Track

Bill Swan

James Lorimer & Company Ltd., Publishers
Toronto, 2003

© 2003 Bill Swan

James Lorimer & Company Ltd. acknowledges the support of the Ontario Arts Council. We acknowledge the support of the Government of Canada through the Book Publishing Industry Development Program (BPIDP) for our publishing activities. We acknowledge the support of the Canada Council for the Arts for our publishing program. We acknowledge the support of the Government of Ontario through the Ontario Media Development Corporation's Ontario Book Initiative.

Cover illustration: Steve Murray

The Canada Council | Le Conseil des Arts
for the Arts | du Canada

ONTARIO ARTS COUNCIL
CONSEIL DES ARTS DE L'ONTARIO

Canada Cataloguing in Publication Data

Swan, Bill, 1939–
    Off track

(Sports stories ; 62)
ISBN 1-55028-807-5 (bound)   ISBN 1-55028-806-7 (pbk.)

I. Title. II. Series: Sports stories (Toronto, Ont.); 62.

PS8587.W338O34 2003   jC813'.54   C2003-904168-9

James Lorimer & Company Ltd.,   Distributed in the United States by:
Publishers   Orca Book Publishers
35 Britain Street   P.O. Box 468
Toronto, Ontario   Custer, WA USA
M5A 1R7   98240-0468
www.lorimer.ca

Printed and bound in Canada.

Contents

Contents

For Joyce, Jim, and Anne.

1

A Failed Test

Tyler Davidson slouched in his seat and ignored his teacher. Outside, in the steaming July heat, a solitary runner ran on the cinder track around the football field.

Tyler's teacher crept up. She stood for a moment by his desk. Tyler knew she was waiting for him to lift his eyes, to admit she was *there*, that he was wasting his time. Wasting everybody's time.

"You didn't do very well this week," the teacher said, gently placing his Friday test paper face-up on the desk. "Not very well indeed."

On the track, the runner completed his two-lap run, checked his watch, and walked in a circle on the infield grass.

Tyler looked down. His paper was blank — except for his name, partially written in thick black letters:

Tyler Davidso

His pencil had broken that morning when he wrote his name: Tyler Davidson. He hadn't bothered to sharpen it, so never did finish the "n."

The only other mark on the paper was a tiny zero in the teacher's tiny hand, with her tiny initials.

She held the paper down with the fingers of one hand. Tyler could tell she was waiting.

"Tyler, I can wait all afternoon. Is this how you want to spend the rest of Friday? A detention would be more fun."

Outside, the runner appeared again on the track, running strong.

The teacher did not move. Her hand remained calmly on the test paper. Finally Tyler lifted his eyes.

"Do you want to tell me about it?" the teacher said.

Tyler shrugged.

"Tyler, you've spent a week in class doing little more than writing your name on worksheets. I have a hunch you are capable of more than that."

"Ain't nothing to tell."

Her name was Ms Ramsahai. She had black hair almost to her shoulders, and deep brown eyes. She was dressed for summer school: jeans, a golf shirt, and running shoes.

Finally, she removed her hand from the paper. Tyler grabbed it and stuffed it into the bottom of his backpack.

"There is much to tell, Tyler," she said. "We've finished one week out of six in this course. Unless you show that you can do this work soon, you are doomed."

Tyler gave a small gesture with his shoulders and the corners of his mouth, like a mini-shrug. It meant: "Who cares?"

Ms Ramsahai sat on the desk in front of him, grasped her knee in her hands, and smiled.

"Tyler, I care. Nobody fails a course I teach. But you have to not only show that you can do the work. You have to *do* the work."

He waited. He knew there would be more.

"So how long are you going to keep this up?" she asked softly.

Tyler stood, leaning all his weight on his left hip. First his father had forced him to go to summer school. Yanked him out of baseball and soccer. Cut him off the Internet. Unplugged his computer. Now this teacher wanted to *help*.

"Weren't my idea."

"Look, Tyler, I don't know what's going on at home that has you acting this way. Would it help if I spoke to your parents?"

Tyler shifted. Much his mother cared. She was in Halifax with that job.

"Nothing more they can take away," Tyler replied.

"We'll think of that as a last resort. For now, this is between you and me, Tyler. You know what you have to do. And I know you can do it. But I really don't think you want to accumulate any more Friday tests like this."

He didn't have words for any of this; he didn't try to form any. The message was the predictable teacher's message. "If you want to do well …" Blah, blah, blah. Sure.

Holding his backpack by one strap from his shoulder, he sighed.

Finally, Ms Ramsahai asked: "Is there anything I can do to help you through this?"

The silence was broken by the grating noise from the electric clock. Outside, he could hear a bicycle tire crunching on the cinder track. He drew another deep breath and expelled it impolitely.

"Can I go now?"

He shuffled out of the classroom. In the hallway, he kicked the release bar of the side door open and stepped into the sunshine.

The sun and a stray breeze were refreshing after a morning in a closed classroom. At the edge of the track, the runner knelt by the triangular frame of an upside-down bicycle. He spun the rear wheel, made adjustments, spun it some more.

Up close, the runner looked smaller than he had on the track. He was older than Tyler, perhaps fifteen but, surprisingly, shorter. His close-cropped hair was dark blond or light brown.

He wore a Raptors jersey and shorts. He glistened with sweat.

Tyler glanced once or twice at him. He didn't bother to speak. He still did not feel like speaking to anyone.

"Hand me that wrench, would ya?"

Tyler turned toward the voice, even pointed to his own chest and mimed, "Me?" But he didn't say it out loud.

"Yeah. That one. On the ground beside you."

Tyler looked down. He picked up the wrench.

"Thanks. I'm just tuning up the bike. I'm running a triathlon a week tomorrow."

Tyler felt dumb, sucked into a conversation, yet still fascinated by this older boy. He had an animated look; a jock, Tyler thought, and that made him different from anyone else he had seen at summer school.

"Tri …" It was a big word, and Tyler did not feel comfortable with big words.

"Triathlon. Swim. Bike. Run."

"Yeah?"

"You've heard of Simon Whitfield, haven't you?" He said it as though anyone who hadn't heard of Simon Whitfield might be not very bright.

"Oh, yeah. I heard of him." He had, but couldn't remember the details.

The older boy looked up. He smiled a bright, toothy grin.

"It's okay to say you've never heard of him," he said. "A lot of people haven't. He won a gold medal for Canada in the triathlon. In the 2000 Olympics. In Australia."

Tyler now felt mildly uncomfortable. For the first time, he wondered if it wasn't time to return to class.

"Tri … " He still couldn't get the word right.

"Tri, as in tricycle," the runner said. "Means three. You know: three wheels on the trike …"

"I'm not that dumb."

"Yeah, right. Any of us here in summer school are either dumb or didn't pay attention. Besides, dumb means you can't speak. Which you're doing well at. Yeah, three events: Swim, bike, run. One after the other." He paused to wipe sweat from his forehead with his left arm. "It's the toughest sport there is," he said.

Tyler smirked. "Hockey's tough."

"Sure, if you like getting bruised. If you think that's tough. But in hockey you play for a minute then get a rest. That's not tough. Try swimming 1500 metres, biking forty kilometres and then running another ten. Without a rest. That's what Simon did in the Olympics. My dad coaches me. He says Simon is the best."

"You going to do *that*?" Tyler asked.

"Shorter distances. I'm racing in the same races Simon won nine years before he won in the Olympics. Kids of Steel. You heard of that?"

Tyler shrugged and said nothing.

"You in summer school here?"

Tyler nodded.

"Yeah. Well, I flunked grade-ten math. But I'll get it right this time."

"English," Tyler said, for the first time finding someone who might understand. "Been grounded. No soccer, no baseball."

"Cruddy. Better than repeating a year, though. What time is it? You got the time?"

Tyler didn't.

"I gotta see Mr Jenkins before he gets away."

"Your class over?"

"I got out at noon. That's when I normally come down here to do my track workout."

"I watched ya."

"It's math. I just didn't pay attention in class last year. And

fractions give me a pain. Who'da thought that grade-six fractions would bother me in grade ten? My name's Kevin."

"Mine's Tyler." It felt strange trading names like grown-
ups. At school that wasn't necessary.

"Okay, see you around, eh?" Kevin stood his bicycle up,
wheeled it to the nearest rack, and locked it.

"Can you see that from your class?"

"What? The track? Yeah."

"No. The bicycle rack."

Tyler looked at the bicycle rack and the classroom window,
where Ms Ramsahai stood in the window watching. "Yeah, I
guess."

Kevin looked up at the window. "That your class? Mine's
on the opposite side of the school. If you can see this, then next
week I'll park my bike here and you can keep an eye on it.
Okay? Even with a lock on it there's always some dumb dork
ready to do something."

Tyler thought that would be okay. He didn't have anything
to do in class anyway. Watching a bike locked to a rack would
be exciting.

Summer classes for all grades were held at the local high
school next to the Courtice Community Centre. Any other time
Tyler might have been thrilled to be at the high school, with its
two gyms, a greenhouse and, somewhere he had been told, a
climbing wall.

When Tyler looked up to check the line of sight from his
classroom, he could still see Ms Ramsahai.

"Guess I'd better go," Kevin said.

2

Hidden Card

After class Tyler walked home from school in the July sun and wished that he lived on another planet.

Ms Ramsahai insisted on poking into stuff that was none of her business. As if his father would relent. The more he thought about it, the more angry he became.

It wasn't fair.

The week before he had tried his best to keep his report card from his father. He had known, from the time his teacher had handed it to him, that it held bad news. For two days he kept it in the bottom of his backpack. On the third day Stu Shearer's father boasted that Stu had earned straight A's on his seventh-grade report.

Tyler's father had then asked Tyler where his report card was. It didn't take him long to find it, stuffed in his backpack under a science text and a spare running shoe. The next thing Tyler knew his father was standing by his computer in the basement, waving the report card and talking loudly.

He was a tall man, his long arms in a crisply ironed shirt. He was precise and thorough in everything he did and expected the same of everyone else.

"You know what this means, don't you?" Tyler's father asked.

Tyler hung his head. It was a topic he did not want to discuss. Ever.

"It means first of all: No baseball. No soccer. No sports. Period," his father said, flattening his hands like a baseball umpire calling safe. Tyler didn't feel safe.

"But …"

"Don't 'but' me. It also means summer school. Wherever we can get you in. Either summer school or private tutoring, whatever it takes. You're not going into grade eight with a report like this."

"Dad, the report says I can go into grade eight. It just says I'll need help next year. So I'll catch up. It'll just …"

"And you'll catch up on the grade-seven material and a year from now still be a year behind," his father insisted. "One summer, two months, is a lot less than one year, twelve months. Or didn't you get that far in math, either?" But that comment bounced off, for Tyler was good in math.

"But summer school, Dad. Summer school sucks, inside all day …"

"And no television."

"But …"

"And no computer. Nada. Nothing. Not until you've proven yourself. Start to give me some good results from summer school and we'll reconsider. Until then, nothing."

"I'll die."

Mr. Davidson stopped waving his arms. "People," he said, "do not die of boredom. They don't do anything with boredom except find something to do."

"No television! Come on, Dad …"

"Don't 'Come on, Dad,' me."

"I'll bet Mom would …" He had been about to say, "… not ground me like that." Then he knew that might not be true.

"Perhaps. But then you'd have to call her to find out, wouldn't you?"

Tyler had not talked to his mother since April, ever since she had moved to Halifax to take that new job.

"But what's there to do?" he said, changing the subject.

"What's to do? Lots. Read, for one thing."

"Can I read anything? Or just the boring stuff? That's what you want, isn't it? To have me read boring stuff until my eyeballs are tapioca." His father's one attempt at making tapioca pudding had once been a family joke.

"Tyler, this is serious stuff. You don't seem to appreciate that. You just can't afford to fall behind now. Not at your age. We gotta get you back on the rails."

Tyler shrugged and glared at his father.

"You can't make me."

It had not been the right thing to say. Three days later, Tyler started summer school in spite of a tantrum, two days of silence, and a vow to never do any classwork, ever. Those three days with no television and no computer had seemed like three months.

* * *

That evening, Tyler's father served dinner as usual in the kitchen. They both sat on blue kitchen stools at the long counter.

"You going to call your mother?"

Tyler shrugged. "She coming back?" he asked. The question had been hanging around for months. Only his anger allowed him to ask it now.

"We've been through this before," his father replied. "Is that what this is all about?"

"Well, is she?"

His father gathered up both plates and scraped the scraps into the garbage.

"Your mother has a unique career opportunity, Tyler. We've

told you all this. This job in Halifax is what she's been aiming at since before you were born. She couldn't miss the chance."

"You getting divorced?"

"Tyler, we have a lot to work through. I know this is not easy. It's hard on all of us. But no, we're not planning to divorce."

"You're separated. Bobby Valentino's parents got separated. Then they got divorced."

"We're separated because your mother's job is in Halifax and mine's right here in Courtice."

"Your clients are in Toronto."

"I can do the work from here at home. Most of it, anyway. That way we can make it work. And we decided ..."

"I didn't have anything to say about it."

His father ignored the quip. "... we decided, your mother and I, that we would not move with you about to go into the eighth grade. It wouldn't be fair. Starting a new school and having to make new friends. Besides, her job is a contract for only one year. We'd all be pretty foolish to sell everything here and move just for one year."

Tyler had heard it all before. He stopped listening.

"... with your peers. Tyler, are you listening?"

"I was supposed to go there for a week," he said.

"Last time you didn't even want to consider that," said Mr Davidson. "Now that you're in summer school and can't go, you want to. Is that it?"

"Would you come?"

"Tyler, we've been over this and over this. That week was the only vacation your mother could get. She's new at that job, remember? And that's one week I can't afford to be away. Are you just trying to be obstinate?"

"I don't know. What's 'obstinate' mean?" He stared at his father.

"Obstinate. That's what you're being right now. Do I take it that you're now talking to your mother? After six weeks? You could call her, you know."

Tyler didn't answer.

His father sighed his own angry sigh and left Tyler to fill the dishwasher.

3

The Bicycle

On Sunday night his mother called from Halifax.

"I'm disappointed," she said, her voice thin from being squeezed through telephone wires. "I had planned for you to come down here for a week before your father came out. I was so looking forward to that."

Tyler mumbled into the phone but what he said did not make sense, even to him.

"What I can't understand is what happened to your school work, Tyler. This thing about summer school …"

"I flunked."

"Pardon?"

"I flunked. That's what happened. So now I've got summer school."

There was a pause before his mother replied. "But why, Tyler? You've always done so well. Especially in math."

"Math's fine. It was English."

"Well that's never been a problem before, either. Help me to understand why."

Now it was Tyler's turn to pause. Why? Hearing his parents arguing, night after night, that was part of why. Knowing his mother was leaving, moving halfway across the country, that was why. Knowing that even though both his mother and his father kept saying they did not plan to divorce, he knew better. And if they didn't care, why should he?

Instead, he said: "I dunno."

"I wish I'd been there to help you with your homework. Was that it? You didn't get your homework done? Remember how I used to sit at the dining-room table with you? Maybe if we'd done that, maybe if I'd been there, this wouldn't have happened."

You could have been here if you wanted to be, Tyler thought.

"And I suppose your father was too busy to help you out. Sometimes I think we made the wrong decision. Did we make the wrong decision, Tyler? We did it for you, you know. We didn't want to be moving just before you started the eighth grade. That would have been so awkward."

"Gotta go."

"Well, I'll see if I can change my week's vacation to August, when you've finished summer school. You and your father can still come down then. At least that'll give us some time together. It's been so difficult …"

"Whatever."

Tyler handed the phone to his father. He stepped out the side door from the kitchen. In the yard, he noticed the paint peeling from the playhouse. Two years ago he and his friends could hang from the open windows and climb on the roof.

When Tyler returned to the kitchen his father sat staring at the wallpaper. Neither spoke.

* * *

Monday morning, at the start of the second week, Tyler left for school a half-hour early.

That surprised his father, after the angry breakfasts of the week before.

Tyler didn't speak all through breakfast. Nobody would have confused him with someone who loved summer school. But at eight-fifteen he slid off his stool at the counter.

"I'll ride my bike. If that's okay."

It was his father's turn to be speechless. His jaw went slack and began working like a hungry goldfish.

Tyler rode through the wooded area to the west of the school, emerging behind the building near the edge of the track. No one was in sight this early in the morning.

At the bicycle rack, he realized he had forgotten his lock. He uttered a word he hoped would have shocked any adult who might have been listening, and he gazed out at the track. Dew glistened off the grass on the field.

Over the fence by the edge of the field a stray dog yelped. Tyler watched cars pulling into the parking lot of the Courtice Community Centre next door.

Just then, Ms Ramsahai came out of the main doors of the community centre. She walked quickly across the parking lot, stepping carefully through the gap in the fence between the centre and the high school.

"Good morning to you," she said as she approached, close enough for Tyler to see that her hair was still damp from her morning shower.

Tyler stifled a "good morning," mumbling something else.

"Glad to see you here," she said, still smiling. "After Friday, I wasn't sure."

"I'm waiting for somebody," Tyler said.

"You can come in now if you wish," Ms Ramsahai said. She pulled a key out of her pocket, unlocked the door, and held it open for a moment.

"If you come in now you'll save yourself a trip," she said. Twice the week before, Tyler had forgotten to prop open the side door when he went out for his break. The door opened from the inside with a safety bar. From the outside, it was locked. That meant he had to walk around the whole school to get in through the main entrance and then back through the long hallways. The high school was large — several times larger than his elementary school.

"Oh, man!" Tyler said. He had no intention of going to class now. He still had, what, ten minutes? But it would take him almost that long to get in by going the long way around.

Ms Ramsahai still held the door. Tyler shook his head.

She shrugged. The door eased closed with a mild squeak.

He turned to see Kevin crossing the football field with a girl. Both were walking their bicycles.

"Hi, Tyler," Kevin said. "How's it goin'?"

Kevin exchanged glances with the girl, who smiled. He took off his helmet, and shook his head as though he had long hair. "I just finished my swim workout. I gotta go to class now."

"I'm Samantha," said the girl, leaning over her bike. She looked at Tyler long enough that he felt tingly. "I'm Kevin's sister." She had short brown hair, was about his age, and was dressed in shorts and T-shirt. A fierce-looking green bicycle helmet hung by its strap from the handlebars of her bike.

"Hi," said Tyler.

"Kevin and I have the same swim coach," said Samantha.

"That your bike?" Kevin asked Tyler.

"Yeah. It's pretty beat up."

"No lock, eh? Not a good idea. Want to share mine?" Without waiting for a reply, he draped his chain through the frames of both bicycles and snapped the lock closed.

"There. Now Tyler will keep an eye out all morning so nobody bothers our bikes. Won't you, Tyler?"

"What about you?" Tyler said to Samantha. "You got a lock?"

"I'm not going to school. I may be back later."

She smiled at Tyler. Tyler smiled back.

Kevin glanced at his watch and bounded up the few steps to the door.

"It's locked," Tyler said. "We have to go around."

"Only two minutes until class starts. We don't have time to go around. Crap, I can't afford to be late. I've got a test on triangles."

Samantha brushed by him. "That's okay," she said. "I'll get you in." She walked along the side the building and rapped on the window of Tyler's classroom.

Ms Ramsahai appeared, barely visible through the window glass that reflected visions of the track and football field.

She smiled widely at Samantha, who waved her arms and pointed to the door.

A few seconds later Ms Ramsahai pushed the door open.

"Thanks, Ms Ramsahai," Kevin said.

"You coming in, Samantha?" Ms Ramsahai asked. Samantha shook her head. "I'm going to the library for the morning," she said. "See you guys."

Kevin slipped through the open door. Tyler followed.

"Thanks," he said to Ms Ramsahai. He almost meant it.

4

Guard Duty

All that morning, Tyler kept one eye on the two bicycles chained together outside the classroom window. It required little effort. He sat with arms folded, a blank sheet of paper on the desk in front of him.

Meanwhile, Ms Ramsahai insisted on asking him questions.

"What does this mean for subject-verb agreement, Tyler?"

At each question, Tyler shrugged. Despite the teacher's persistence, Tyler found himself beginning to respect Ms Ramsahai.

At the end of class, Kevin appeared in the doorway.

"Hey, man, wanna get your bike?"

Tyler turned and looked at Ms Ramsahai.

"Class is dismissed," she said. "And don't forget, Tyler; I need that essay. The outline is due Thursday."

"Essay?"

"On the challenge you would like to meet." She smiled. "The outline is due on Thursday. The final version is due at the end of class next Monday. We spent half an hour discussing that this morning. Were you daydreaming all that time?"

Tyler didn't reply.

Outside, Samantha stood by the rack while Kevin spun the dial on his lock and freed the bicycles.

"We're riding," he said, gesturing toward Samantha and

himself. "Want to join us?"

Tyler hesitated. "I'd never keep up. You're a racer."

"Naw. We're both running a triathlon on Saturday, so we're cutting back on training. Today is just a half-hour bike ride. We'll tool along. As long as *you* promise not to race."

Samantha smiled.

"Deal."

Tyler had really wanted to ride with Kevin. In fact, he had devised his whole plan for the day, riding his bicycle to school, with the idea of getting a chance to run — or bike — with the older boy.

"Let's go!"

They rode easily along the uneven path through the wooded area to the west of the school, emerging single-file on Nash Road, almost in front of the school. From there, they headed west to Trull's Road and turned north. Kevin led. Samantha rode behind Tyler.

"You're not going to do the mountain, are you?" Tyler called.

They had quickly passed the subdivisions and the fire hall. Soon they were in open country.

"You want to? Bet you can't make it to the top without walking."

Tyler looked ahead.

At Pebblestone Road, there was a stop sign and a Super-Mailbox. Eight hundred metres further north the Trull's Road Mountain loomed.

Starting from a dip in a gully, the road rose steeply for about the length of a football field. Then the slope eased off, but continued to rise for another 200 metres.

Kevin stopped near the base of the hill.

"You sure you're up to it?" Samantha asked. "It's pretty steep. I don't think we should be doing this one. Not this close to a race."

"It's a good climb," Tyler said.

"Samantha's right. We're racing Saturday, and we should just bike easily. But we do have six more days …"

"Five," said Samantha, counting off the days on her fingers. "Today is Monday. Tuesday, Wednesday, Thursday, Friday, Saturday. Five."

"Okay, five."

Kevin turned to Tyler. "You know Noah Meyers?"

"Nope."

"He's in college now. But he used to run up this hill lots of times. He lived here in Courtice, too. Went to high school here."

Tyler shrugged.

"Not too many people have heard of him. He won the provincial title in the 1500-metres a few years ago," said Kevin.

A car appeared at the top of the hill. It hesitated, then accelerated down toward them.

"Look at that car. They all do that: slow down at the top and then coast down. My dad says this hill's steep enough that a car can get up to ninety, coasting. Think of the fun we'll have coming back down." He smiled.

"Let's go."

Tyler looked down at Kevin's bike. It had sprockets at the front and back, and twelve gears — one for every occasion. Samantha's was similar.

Tyler's department-store dirt bike, on the other hand, had a heavy frame, wide seat, thick handlebars, and only five speeds, each of which made a loud clunking noise when he changed gears.

One minute up the hill, Tyler was standing up on his pedals, gritting out the climb. Kevin stood up, pumped methodically, and was soon several metres ahead.

Samantha attempted to ride behind Tyler. But soon she, too,

moved quietly past him on the left. Tyler continued to stand on his pedals, gritting his teeth. His bicycle continued to move forward, though just barely.

Tyler looked ahead. Kevin stood on his pedals and brought his bike to a standstill without losing balance. He looked back and yelled encouragement: "Keep coming. You're almost past the worst part."

Tyler continued to pump, his bike in the lowest of its five gears. Just when he thought he would have to quit, the slope eased off slightly.

"Now see if you've got any legs left," Kevin yelled.

Tyler rose higher on his pedals and gained some speed.

The slope of the hill had eased, but it was still steep. The lower portion of the hill had been *really* steep.

"You can do it. Come on!" Kevin waited at the top of the hill. "Pump … pump … pump … pump."

Tyler continued, his heavy legs quivering slightly. Completing each stroke now took all of his effort.

"You're almost there!" yelled Samantha.

"Pump … pump … pump … pump."

Kevin called out the numbers of Tyler's down strokes: "Six … five … four … three …"

"Made it!" yelled Tyler when he reached Kevin and Samantha at the top. "I've never biked up this hill before."

"And you did it on that old clunker, too," Kevin said. "If you can take that hill, you can bike anywhere."

"Sure you don't want to try racing a triathlon?" asked Samantha.

Tyler was sure she was kidding.

5

Tyler Sets a Goal

That evening, Tyler sat down across from his father on the patio. Samantha's quip about the triathlon was still on his mind. His father rattled his newspaper, cleared his throat several times, and finally turned to his son.

"Yes?" he said, lowering the newspaper just enough to make eye contact. "What is it?"

Tyler leaned forward over the patio table, put one fist on top the other, and rested his chin on it. "Can I run a triathlon?" he asked.

His father lowered the newspaper even further and folded it carefully. "That's a big undertaking," he said. "Why, the Ironman Triathlon in Hawaii ends with a forty-two kilometre run. After the biking and swimming."

"Not that one. Shorter. There's this kid at school—"

"He's running one?"

"That's what he said. He rides his bike at school. And runs on the track."

"Well, it sounds as though he's preparing himself. Which, if you remember, is why you are at summer school. So if this is an attempt to get around the ban on sports, the answer is no."

"But I haven't asked yet."

"You asked if you could run a triathlon. I said the ban on sports is still in place."

Tyler leaned back in his chair and exhaled, slowly. "I didn't say I wanted to run one tomorrow," he said. "I just meant, could I? Some day?"

"Well, your first objective is this English class," his father replied. "Once you pass that, the answer will be 'yes.' Of course, you could go back to baseball and soccer, then, too."

"They'll both be over."

"Hmm. Did you have a specific race in mind?"

"Not really. Something nearby. If I could go on the Internet I could find …"

At that, his father shook his head from side to side. "No, no, no, no. You're off the computer and the Internet completely until this course is over."

Tyler sat deflated in the chair, arms hanging loosely. He thought of Samantha, and of riding with her and Kevin. It had been fun. But the English course bothered him. Even though he had done no work in class, Ms Ramsahai still bugged him as though he might actually *do* something. What was it she had said that day? About a *challenge* essay?

"But I have an essay to write," Tyler said, sitting up quickly.

"An essay?"

"Yeah. On a challenge. Something difficult we would like to do. I gotta get the outline in by Thursday. And to do that I gotta do some research."

"There's books for research."

"The essay needs up-to-date research. Come on, Dad. A couple nights on the Internet and I'll have everything I need." He hesitated for a moment and added, "Along with what I find in the library, too."

"What are you writing the essay on?" his father asked.

"Um," Tyler said, thinking quickly, "triathlons."

"Triathlons?"

"It has to be about a challenge I would like to take on."

His father picked up the newspaper and opened it again. "Maximum two hours," he said. "Tonight and tomorrow night only."

Tyler pumped his left fist under the table out of sight, whispered "Yes!" and bounded out of the chair.

"Thanks, Dad," he said.

"Don't forget to call your mother," his father said, as though that were the answer to everything.

* * *

Tyler showed up for school next day at eight-fifteen. He locked his bike to the stand and walked out to the track, kicking at the cinders. He squinted to line up the football goalposts. He drew a line on the cinder track to mark the spot.

Quickly, he looked around. He could see no one. Next door, at the community centre, cars entered and left the parking lot. Parents were dropping off their children at the daycare.

Tyler dropped into a kneeling sprinter's starting position. Tensing his muscles, he lurched forward, running hard along the straightaway. Breathless, he pulled up as the track curved left past the goal line.

Sheepishly, he looked up to see if anyone had watched. Nobody. He walked around the curve of the track. When he was even with the goalposts, he dropped again into the sprinter's starting position. Then: Bang! He was off again.

His muscles felt taut from the bicycle hill climb the day before. But running felt good. He enjoyed feeling the wind on his face, the crunch of cinders under his feet.

He wondered then about Kevin and Samantha and the triathlon. Swimming. Bicycling. Running. All in one race. He wondered how that would feel, to tire muscles in one event and then turn to another.

And what kind of running? Not likely sprinting. Tyler recalled his 1500-metre race — the metric mile — earlier that spring. For that, and even longer distances, you don't crouch into the starter's block. So he thought it might be the same for the triathlon, but he didn't know. None of the Web sites he had visited the night before, when his father wasn't looking, showed runners starting.

He had learned plenty about triathlons on the Web. He learned about the Ironman Triathlon in Hawaii. About the first swim-bike-run race in the 1970s; about the triathlon in the Olympics.

He discovered that there was a Canadian series for young triathletes called Kids of Steel, and he learned that Simon Whitfield won the Ontario championship in 1991 — and nine years later won an Olympic gold medal.

He looked across the football field to the community centre. In addition to the library, a gymnasium, and the daycare, the centre also had a swimming pool with a corkscrew slide and a wading pool for toddlers.

Tyler crossed the wet grass at the edge of the football field, ducked through the gap in the fence, and stepped onto the parking lot.

He pulled the front door open and entered. He could see the pool through the glass wall straight ahead. Several swimmers thrust their arms through the water, while at the pool's end a woman in a swimsuit with a peaked visor on her head held a clipboard in one hand and a whistle in the other. Her loud voice bounced off the pool walls and echoed into the foyer.

To his right, a clerk at the information desk shuffled papers, answered the phone, and responded to questions from two girls

— seemingly all at the same time. Behind a concrete pillar, Tyler could see that the snack bar was open, too, with two tables off to one side.

A poster was taped to the pillar:

Triathlon!
Saturday, August 21.
Courtice Community Centre!
All age groups. Boys and girls
Ages 5–7, 8–9, 10–11, 12–13, 14–15, 16–19.
Advanced registration only, $25.

August 21. That was five weeks away.

He was now in his second week of summer school, and his father had not relented. Tyler was still not allowed to play soccer or baseball. No TV or computer.

Five weeks was a long time. Would his father allow him to enter a race? After summer school was over? Not if he didn't pass, he thought. For the first time, he started to look beyond the pain of summer classes.

Tyler sat on the bench in front of the glass wall overlooking the pool, put his chin in his hands, and stared vacantly.

The woman beside him touched his arm and pointed. A swimmer on the pool deck rapped on the glass two metres in front of him.

"That guy wants to get your attention."

Tyler looked. Kevin rapped again lightly, dripping wet in his swimming trunks.

"See you at one!" Kevin said, mouthing the words with emphasis in case the glass blocked the sound. But Tyler could hear clearly. They would ride again that day. Tyler was pleased.

"At one!" Kevin yelled, exaggerating his mouth movements.

Tyler held up his index finger. Kevin replied with a thumbs-up.

By the pool, the woman with the clipboard and visor blew her whistle, and a gaggle of shivering young swimmers gathered around her. Kevin waved and walked barefoot on the pool apron toward the change room.

Tyler wandered back to the pillar and looked again at the poster. August 21. A triathlon. Swim, bike, run. Summer school would be over. Surely his father would have unlocked his jail door by then.

The swimmers splashed and yelled in the pool. Tyler turned back to the poster, reading it again. He walked over to the desk and picked up a brochure with an entry form.

Swim, 150 metres; bicycle, ten kilometres; run, two kilometres.

He heard footsteps behind him, and turned just in time to see Ms Ramsahai coming down the hall from the library.

6

Teacher Talk

"Planning a race, Tyler?" Ms Ramsahai said. "Or just picking a topic for your challenge essay?"

Tyler shrugged.

"Maybe," he said, turning back to the pool.

"Your friend Kevin is well into triathlons," the teacher continued. "I came out to watch him last year when he did the race here."

Tyler brightened in spite of himself. "I went biking yesterday with Kevin," he said. "Up Trull's Road Mountain." He saw from the look on her face that she did not know about the mountain.

"The big hill," he added. "Up Trull's Road. With Kevin and Samantha."

Ms Ramsahai laughed. "I've never heard it called a mountain before," she said. "But it certainly would be a challenge on a bicycle."

Tyler smiled.

Ms Ramsahai jerked her head toward the main door. "It's time to head to class now," she said. "Want to walk over with me?"

Tyler took one last look at the the pool, wondering where Kevin had gone. And he hadn't seen Samantha, either.

"Okay," he said. Without turning, he pointed again to the

bottom of the poster. "What's that mean?" he asked. "Advanced registration only? Does that mean you have to enter ahead of time?"

"Yes. Race organizers like to know how many racers they're dealing with. Some smaller races still accept race-day entries, though."

"I see."

"The triathlon would make a good topic for your essay on challenges," she continued as they walked toward the high school.

"I did some research last night. On the Internet," Tyler replied.

"That's the goal of the assignment — to get you thinking about how you would deal with a big challenge. And a triathlon is a *big* challenge."

"I'm not sure about writing on triathlons. Writing takes the fun out of stuff. You know."

"I hate to act the teacher on you before class starts," said Ms Ramsahai with a laugh, "but an essay is just like a triathlon. The tough part is the preparation."

"Preparation?"

"Don't tell me you zoned out while I was talking about that, too, Tyler!" She laughed aloud but somehow Tyler knew she wasn't laughing at him. "Tyler, Tyler, Tyler, you have caterpillars in your head. If you were going to run a triathlon, you would have to train for it. The same with an essay. Anything you do to get ready to write it is preparation. It's called pre-writing."

"Like sharpening pencils?" Tyler was trying to be funny, but the question came out as serious. Worse, dumb.

"Yes, like sharpening pencils."

"Research?"

"And research. Oh, Tyler, we've got so much work to do

with you," said Ms Ramsahai. "We really do. Don't worry so much about writing that essay. Use your head. Think. What do you need to know before you try to race in a triathlon?"

They had crossed the parking lot, stepped through the gap in the fence, and reached the edge of the track.

"Don't know," said Tyler.

"How can you find out?"

"Well," he said, his voice almost returning to the insolence he had shown up to now. "Kevin could tell me lots. Samantha, too." He said it with pride, as though he had evaded a teacher trap. "They both run triathlons."

"Very good. Anywhere else?"

"I dunno. I found a lot on the Internet. My dad let me back on just to do research."

"That it?"

"Maybe the library. Maybe there's a book on it some-where," he said, almost sheepishly.

"Could be," said the teacher.

"And if you found out this information, do you think you could write it down for me by Thursday?"

"The essay?"

"No, the outline. You really did zone out on me yesterday, didn't you?" Ms Ramsahai unlocked the back door of the high school. "If you're thinking of running a triathlon, you will have to gather all of the information anyway. We're going to cover the writing part in class this morning. If you have to do a writ-ten report anyway, you might as well do it on something that turns your crank."

"Turns your crank?" asked Tyler. Was this teacher for real, he wondered.

"It was my grandfather's expression. A hundred years ago, cars and tractors didn't have electric starters. The driver had to get out and turn a crank at the front of the vehicle to start it. Anything that turns your crank is anything that gets you started, gets you interested."

She paused for a moment as they entered the classroom. "My own theory is that you cannot do anything well unless it 'turns your crank.'"

Later, as the other students entered class, Tyler realized he had not only arrived early, but had arrived first. Only then did he look out the window and see Kevin ride over from the community centre and park his bike in the rack. He could see also Samantha riding out the drive.

The lesson that morning focused on the writing of the report. Ms Ramsahai talked about changing research into a first draft.

"You will need to say what the challenge is in one sentence," she said. "You need background. Talk to someone who has done the challenge. Quote her or him as part of your essay."

"Quote?" someone asked.

"Quote. Use that person's words to help tell the story."

"Isn't that play … I can't remember the word," said one of the boys.

"Plagiarism? Nope. It's plagiarism only if you take something without saying where it came from and try to pass it off as your own."

"Cool."

"And don't forget, we have the usual test on Friday. You might want to try to improve on last week's grade."

Tyler was sure she was looking at him when she made that remark.

* * *

At morning break, Tyler found Kevin near the bike rack.

"Great ride yesterday," Kevin said, smiling.

"Yeah," said Tyler. "That's a huge hill. How was your swim this morning?"

"Great, I stayed to do a few more laps after the coach left. Still on for another ride today?

"Sure." Tyler hesitated. "But no hills, eh? Where's that triathlon on Saturday?"

Kevin nodded. "Lindsay. Four more days. That's why I cut down on my training this week. Samantha was right, that hill yesterday really wasn't a good idea."

"Why not? Wouldn't that toughen you up?"

Kevin smiled. "Coaches don't like it when you do a hard workout right before a race. The last week's supposed to be easier. Maybe short, fast stuff. Dad says that gives the legs some snap. Hard runs and rides tire you out the same as a race."

"Not hill climbs?"

"Wasn't short, wasn't fast."

"I saw the poster about the race here in August," Tyler said. "I'm thinking of doing it."

"The triathlon? Great. I'm going in that one too. How're you training?"

Tyler grinned. "I started yesterday," he said, "with a climb up Trull's Road Mountain."

Kevin laughed. "You've got some time," he said. "I didn't train at all for my first triathlon. Just jumped in and raced."

"How'd you do?"

Before Kevin could answer, something caught his attention. An older male teacher came out of the school door and headed toward the boys. "Uh-oh," said Kevin, "here comes Jenkins. He agreed to help me work on fractions today after classes. Says I should spend most of my time on them because they're my weak spot. I hate fractions."

"Then why volunteer for a detention?"

"Because I need them," Kevin replied. "You can't avoid stuff you hate."

"Whatever." Tyler looked up at the older boy. "How do you train for a triathlon?"

Kevin waved to the teacher. "I'm just going in, Mr Jenkins. Be right there," he said. Then he turned back to Tyler.

"You got three sports, right? Swimming, biking, and running."

"So I do that every day?"

"Naw. Two sports a day at most. Starting out, one's enough. Later you can move on to two — you don't want to wear yourself out. You already ride your bike. And everybody can run. You run, right?"

"I ran the 1500-metres in track."

"Then you'll be fine. Can you swim?"

Tyler swallowed. He could swim, he just wasn't very good at it.

"A bit."

"Okay. You gotta practice, that's all. Hey, I've got an idea! You want to see a triathlon?"

"See one?"

"Yeah, watch. Why don't you come up to Lindsay with us on Saturday? Samantha and I are racing, but you can see how the race works. Like, you've got to see the transition to believe it."

"What's that?"

"When you, you know, come out of the pool and then get on your bike. It's awesome!" By now Kevin was walking backwards, heading for the school and his extra classwork.

"See you at one," he said with a wave.

During the last half of class that day, Tyler took out a blank piece of paper and made a list of what he knew about triathlons and what he had to do to train for one. Near the end of class, Ms Ramsahai walked by. "An excellent list," she said.

"Thanks."

"And your outline shows a good grasp of detail. You're off to a good start."

Not until then did he realize he was actually planning to write his essay. That was the day he started paying attention to his teacher in class.

7

Triathlon Fever

On Tuesday evening, Tyler waited until his father emerged from the den at the end of a day's work.

"Can I use the computer again tonight?" Tyler asked. "I've got more work to do on my essay."

His father looked up the stairs at him and blinked. "How's that?"

"The essay. On triathlons. Remember?" Tyler said.

"I wouldn't think there would be that much on the Internet," his father replied. "But I did say two evenings, didn't I?"

"I gotta type out the outline. Besides, I still have to write it. That'll take a few nights. It's due next Monday. And Dad?"

His father waited.

"On Saturday a guy I met at school, Kevin, is going to Lindsay to race in a triathlon. He invited me to go. To watch. That's what I'm writing my essay on, the triathlon. So that would be research, too. So I really should go, shouldn't I?"

"Go?"

"To Lindsay. For the triathlon. To watch. Saturday. Kevin says it's the toughest sport there is," Tyler added. "But I can't write an essay about that from just a book."

He paused, but just for a moment.

"Can I go? Saturday?"

"Whoa, there. First the computer. You're grounded, remember? Until school's out."

"But I can't write about a triathlon unless I see one."

"I would have thought you'd need to race in one. Then you'd have first-hand experience."

For a moment, Tyler thought this might be the right time to mention the race in August. But he had sprung two surprises on his dad already. A third might be too much.

"Then can I go?"

"Hey, I didn't say that. I just said …"

"Dad, it's research. I'll finish my outline tonight. Tomorrow I'll get started on the essay. But I need to watch the race."

"And when's the essay due?"

Tyler realized his father was just beginning to focus on the request.

"Monday. In class."

Mr Davidson rubbed his chin, trying to make up his mind. Tyler knew the longer he rubbed, the worse his chances were.

"I have to see the transitions to understand them," he said, suddenly.

"Transitions?" his father repeated.

"Yeah. From swimming to biking, then from biking to running. I've read the rules, but I really need to see them done in a race."

His father thought for a moment. "Isn't that where they run a marathon? That seem a bit much for kids."

For that, Tyler was partially prepared, anyway.

"That's the Ironman Triathlon," he said. "Where they do the marathon at the end. Twenty-six miles, that's 42.2 kilometres. See, I've done some work. For kids it's a lot shorter. For my age they swim 150 metres, bike ten kilometres, and run two kilometres. Plus they swim in a pool."

Mr Davidson looked Tyler straight in the eye.

"Okay," he said slowly. "Computer for research. Only on triathlons. And you can go Saturday to watch." Then he added, "For research."

For the first time in months, Tyler wanted to hug his father. He smiled instead.

* * *

Wednesday after school, Tyler met Kevin and Samantha for a ride. They started from the parking lot of the community centre and rode east on Nash Road.

"This is the course the triathlon in August takes," Samantha said. "There's really only one big hill. I wish there were more."

"More hills? That's weird," said Tyler.

"Everybody else poops out on the uphill. That's when I catch them."

Just before they parted after the ride, Kevin rode up beside Tyler.

"My dad entered you in the triathlon on Saturday," he said. "Paid the fees and everything. So now you've gotta do it."

"But why? How? I mean …"

"He misunderstood. He thought you wanted to enter the race, not just watch, so he entered you, along with Sam and me."

"I don't understand. What about the fee?"

"Our treat. We'll even loan you my old bike. You certainly can't race with that old clunker." He pointed at Tyler's cross-country bike, which rattled every time he went over a bump.

"You'll have to get your father's signature on an entry form, but that's about all. My dad couldn't do that part. Just print the form off the Web site, get your dad to sign it, and bring it with you on Saturday."

Tyler didn't know what to say. All he could think of was one word: "Thanks."

That evening, his father emerged from the den only to pay for the pizza he had ordered for dinner.

"Big deadline," he said, retreating back into the den, munching on his double cheese smothered in olives. "It would be a good idea to call your mother."

Half a pizza and two vanilla colas later, Tyler agreed. He thought back to the day when his mother had thunked down the car trunk lid on her suitcase, hugged him, and had kissed him on both cheeks. He watched her back out of the driveway.

For the first time since then he felt less angry. He dialled his mother's number on the kitchen phone.

Two rings later: "Hello."

"I'm doing an essay on triathlons," he said, without introduction. "And guess what? On Saturday I'm going to race in one!"

His mother paused. "Race in one? Your father mentioned about your going to watch one. In Lindsay, wasn't it? You're not taking on too much, are you, with baseball, and soccer?"

"Mom, Dad grounded me from those two."

"He said you were going to watch."

"I was going to. Then today Kevin asked me if I wanted to run in it. Said his dad made the arrangements by mistake. So I thought, hey, I'm going to be there anyway so why not? Running the race would be even better research than watching it, don't you think? It's going to be super-cool."

"Well, just you don't overdo it. And be careful."

"Mom, I'm gonna be fine. Are you gonna be fine? Are you and Dad getting divorced?"

He didn't know why he asked that question. A long silence followed.

"Your dad said you asked him that, too. No, Tyler, we're not getting divorced. I don't know where you got that idea."

"I heard you fight. Before you left. And then you left."

His mother sighed. "Tyler, we didn't fight. We discussed things loudly. There's a difference."

Now it was Tyler's turn to be silent.

"Tyler? You still there? Put your father on." Then, almost as an afterthought, she added, "I love you, Tyler."

Tyler put the receiver down on the kitchen counter.

"Dad!" he yelled. "Mom's on the phone."

The red extension light came on as his father picked up the phone. Tyler slipped out the kitchen door, onto the patio. He could hear their tiny voices in the receiver as though they were both a galaxy away.

8

The Triathlon

Tyler shivered by the edge of the pool. Voices echoed off the high ceiling and tiled walls. Around him, other runners, also dressed only in swim trunks, shook out nervous legs.

Just then, Kevin appeared beside him.

"Remember, six laps," he said. "That's up the pool and back, up the pool and back, up the pool and back."

"I can count to six," said Tyler with a nervous smile. "It's English I failed, not math."

"Whatever. I'll be with dad and Sam, out by the exchange area. When you come out of the pool, head for the bicycles. Where I showed you. Then you bike ten kilometres to the park. Just follow the others. When you get to the park the marshals will tell you where to run."

"What about you and Sam?"

"Our races are later. We may see you at the end."

"So I wear my bathing suit for the whole race?"

"Yeah. Out of the pool you'll need to put on shoes, throw on a T-shirt, grab your helmet …"

"Helmet! I don't have a helmet!"

"Relax. We brought one of my old ones. If you get on your bike without a helmet you'll be disqualified. So don't forget. And do up the strap before you grab the bike or you'll be out, too."

"Helmet."

"Right. And no riding in the exchange area."

"No riding?"

"Pull the bike out of the rack and walk it out of the exchange. There'll be a line on the road. It's to keep people from running over each other."

"Sure."

A race official with a clipboard herded the competitors to the far end of the pool. "Six to a heat," said the official. "Boys twelve and thirteen, two heats."

Tyler stood at the edge of the pool in Lane 6.

"Mark!"

Tyler moved his toes to the ledge and looked sideways down the line. Bending his knees, he held both of his arms back and tried to look like the others, even if he was unsure of what he was doing. For a moment he wished his father hadn't signed the forms.

The swimmers froze in position. Silence.

At the whistle, Tyler lurched into the pool, attempting a starting dive. But instead he smacked a stinging belly flop, and when he regained his senses, he was in the churning pool, half-choking as he tried to keep his face clear of the turbulence made by the swimmer in the next lane.

Tyler swallowed water and sputtered, but arm over arm he began to recover some of the space between himself and the next swimmer.

At the first turn, he touched the wall just ahead of his rival. Briefly he stood, and threw himself back down the pool, realizing that the lead swimmers were already halfway back on the second lap. Even his rival in the next lane had somehow sped by him.

Tyler took all this in at a glance. Head down, he changed his stroke and swam with his head underwater. Stroke, stroke, stroke, stroke. Four. He pulled his head up to breathe and inhaled water.

Coughing, he continued until he felt the pool's end. Two laps. Four more to go.

He hit the turnaround, placed his feet against the end of the pool, and shoved. The effort pushed him two body lengths ahead, almost catching the closest swimmer.

Determined, he put his head down, working his arms overhand. One, two, three, four. His father had once tried to teach him a proper crawl, popping his head up every third stroke to breathe. Back then it had seemed too much trouble. He wished now that he had listened.

His arms began to feel heavier. He needed air. He slowed his stroke and pulled his head out to one side for a breath.

One wasn't enough. He held his head up, sucking in air. It interfered with his stroke. His chest rose higher in the water and he could feel himself slow.

At the pool's end this time, he paused to wipe his eyes before jumping back in. Already, one length away, one swimmer was out of the water and heading outdoors.

He turned at lap four to continue the last two lengths. He found himself alone in a very quiet pool.

His rubbery arms quivered and he had no strength. His lungs hurt; his eyes smarted. His hands splashed into the water. To keep going required all of his effort.

Had it not been for Kevin and his father, Tyler would have quit.

"That's the finish," said an official in a quiet voice when Tyler touched in. "Out the door, to the right."

Tyler glanced once about him. The people on the apron of the pool stood frozen. The next heat of swimmers were statues.

The officials were statues. When Tyler tried to lift himself from the pool he felt, too, like a statue.

"Come on, son," said the official. "Next leg. Out the door, to the right."

He half rolled onto the pool apron. Dripping, he headed for the white July light of the open door. Someone handed him a towel. His bare feet slapped on the sun-heated pavement between a row of pylons.

Wobbling blindly, Tyler sought out the bicycle rack where Kevin and his father had placed Kevin's old bike. Their shouts from the other side of the crowd barrier helped him to find it.

"To the left!" Kevin shouted. "Left! Other left!"

The exchange area was a battle zone. Discarded towels hung loosely over bike racks. Two racers still scrambled frantically to put on their shoes. Parents and friends of runners, barred from helping in the exchange area, yelled encouragement and advice from beyond the fence.

He finished what drying he could, discarded the towel and sat down on the pavement by the bike, trying to pull on the socks. His still-damp feet resisted, but he finally managed to roll them on. He jammed his feet into his running shoes — the worn, battered ones whose laces had not been undone since the day he got them. Then he pulled the T-shirt, which was plenty large enough, over his head. The helmet went on easily but he couldn't do up the chin strap.

"Hold still," said race attendant, who stepped up and snapped the strap into place.

"You're all set," she said.

"Go get 'em!" yelled Kevin.

Tyler grabbed the bike and started to throw one leg over the seat.

"Walk it!" shouted Kevin. "Walk to the yellow line!"

Tyler flashed a smile. Holding the bike by the seat and the handlebars, he pushed it from the exchange area between a line of traffic cones. At the street, a thick yellow line marked the beginning of the bicycle course.

"Go!" yelled Samantha. "Go, go, go!

He threw one leg over the crossbar and extended it until he pressed against the pedal. Down the street, he could see two more bicycles. At least some were still in sight.

His wet bathing suit clung to the seat. He lifted himself onto his toes, powering with his legs to gain speed. He felt more comfortable on the bike than he had in the pool.

The two bikers ahead had emerged from the pool a full minute ahead of Tyler, but had wasted time in the exchange. He aimed for the nearest one by focusing his eyes on the back of the boy's shirt.

He gained slowly on the first straightaway. At the corner, he timed his turn to pull inside, gaining a full bike length. Not last place, he thought, as he crept by his target.

The next biker was further ahead. Tyler rose onto his toes, pumping full speed on the straightaway. He caught the next rider on the corner, this time swinging wide as the other biker tried to keep to the inside.

Tyler leaned forward and dropped his chin near the handlebars as he had seen the others do. There were six boys in his heat, and two were behind him. That put him in fourth — definitely not last.

In the distance, the third-place biker rolled on with little effort. Tyler was tired. The idea of racing ten kilometres tired him even more. On one long downhill stretch he could see, far ahead, the three leading bikes. It took all of his effort just to keep going.

Tyler saw a big number five painted on an orange traffic cone. A woman marshal waved him on.

"Five kilometres! Halfway! You're looking good!"

Tyler gasped. His legs felt like rubber — and he still had to run!

He gained speed on the downhill and swung wide around the third corner. The course started to level out. Twice he glimpsed the other racers. He dared not look back to see who was following.

A big number nine marked the last kilometre. He had been cycling alone for a long time.

Tyler pumped hard up the last hill toward the park entrance, dismounted at the finish line, and followed the official's pointing finger.

"Bikes and helmets on the rack," he called. "Follow the markers!"

Kevin appeared on the other side of the fence, shouting something he couldn't hear. Tyler pushed the bike to the proper rack, stood it upright, took off his helmet, and hung it over the seat.

A volunteer in the exchange area looked down at Tyler's old tattered shoes. "Follow the trail there, left at the trees."

Suddenly Tyler felt very alone. He started to jog, but his leg muscles, tightened from the bike, refused. He tottered. He looked around, confused. Behind him, racers were entering the exchange area. Ahead, the trees marked the running trail. One runner plodded up a hill to his right. Further up, two others seemed to move in slow motion, as though underwater.

Two kilometres.

After the first dozen steps his legs lost their wobble, and he fell into an even pace on the uphill.

"Way to go! Way to go!" he heard someone yell from behind a tree.

He turned right onto a slight upgrade. He shortened his steps, plugging up it. At the top, the course turned to the right again, still rising toward its crest.

When his legs felt their heaviest and his lungs began to burn again, Tyler looked up to try to see the top of the hill. That's when he saw the third runner.

Walking.

Tyler continued, his steps dogged, determined — but slow. If the other runner was walking that meant he was gaining!

Soon, the third-place runner was only metres ahead. When Tyler reached the top of the hill, he could see that the course sloped sharply downhill. The walker had begun to run again.

Samantha leaned over the snow fence at the side of the course. "Get him now!" she yelled. "Looking good! Take him!"

The downhill gave Tyler new energy. More people were gathered along this section of the course, yelling and cheering. He rose onto his toes and propelled himself down the slope, his elbows out for balance.

At the bottom he caught the runner. The course turned right, then right again.

Third!

Now he could see the finish line across the rolling park. Determined to look good in this last stretch, he flew over the grass, powering up the final rise to where the pylons funnelled him toward the finish. Third! He couldn't believe it. The other two had finished now — no one else was in sight. Not bad for a first triathlon, he thought.

He didn't hear the footsteps until the other runner pulled up beside him. He recognized him as the first guy he had passed on the bicycle leg. Disbelieving, he tried to respond, pumping his arms and trying to lift his exhausted legs in an all-out sprint.

It was too late.

He was running uphill on uneven turf. His legs had nothing

left to offer. The other runner continued past. Tyler, drained, sweating, and exhausted, followed across the finish line two steps behind for fourth place in Heat One.

He dropped to his knees and drank in air.

"Welcome to the triathlon," said Kevin, smiling, as he and Samantha helped him walk through the park. "Now we've got to go get ready for our races."

Tyler bought an orange juice and sat in the shade of a butternut tree, wondering if he would have the energy to cheer his friends through their races. He was still sitting there when the winner of the second heat of twelve- to thirteen-year-old boys surged across the finish line. He didn't even look tired.

9

A Lesson

First thing Monday morning, Tyler marched up to Ms Ram-sahai's desk, handed her his completed essay, and smiled.

"You're early," she said, smiling back. "We are going to work on this in class."

"I ran the triathlon," Tyler said.

"That's great!" said the teacher. "You are getting into some pretty detailed research. How did you do?"

"At the race or with the essay?"

"With the race," she replied. "You did well on the running part, I've heard," she said.

"I thought my legs were going to fall off," Tyler said. "When I started to run after biking I couldn't even get started."

"That happens, I'm told."

"But I passed one runner. For a while I was third in my heat."

"How was the swimming?"

Tyler frowned. "Brutal," he said. "I thought I could swim. But I've never gone that far — just across the pool, stuff like that."

"That was your first long swim?" asked the teacher.

"It was tough. I was a lap behind everybody else. And the exchange!"

"Tricky?"

"There were two others who had never done it before, either," Tyler said. "They got out ahead of me on the swim, but I caught them on the biking part."

"That must have felt good."

"It's hard on the legs when you've got people so far ahead of you."

"Sounds as though you could use some conditioning. And perhaps some skill building."

"Skill building?" Tyler asked.

"Skills. Like swimming — sounds as though you need some training there."

"And exchanges. I'm going to practice those, you can bet on it."

"I wouldn't worry too much about the brickwork until you've got some endurance training down," said Ms Ramsahai.

"Brickwork?"

"The exchanges. The exchange from swimming to the bike. And from the bike to running. You didn't see that word in your research?"

"Oh, yeah. Kevin mentioned it," he said. "Kevin won his race. And Samantha was second. She's good. You know Samantha?"

"I know Sam," said Ms Ramsahai.

"She's good. She beat me. She can really swim. Wish I could swim like that."

"Well, it sounds as though you've had a good introduction. I look forward to reading your essay. You going to do this again?"

"The essay?"

"No, Tyler, the triathlon. You were eyeing that poster last week. I just wondered if the experience had changed your mind."

"No way! I'm doing the one in August, for sure. I've got stuff to work on now. Kevin and Samantha said I can train with them."

"Well, now you have a focus. If you'll give me a few minutes at the beginning of class to read your essay, we'll see where you can begin to build some skills there, too."

Tyler looked down at the paper he had handed her. "But it's done," he said, some of the pride gone from his voice. "I finished it. Yesterday. At home."

Other students now began to file into the room. "I appreciate that," said Ms Ramsahai. "Tyler, nothing is ever done until it's a good as it can be. I'll just look for things you could fix up in class that will give you a better mark."

Tyler shrugged. He had finished the essay. Wasn't that enough?

"Tyler, marks do count. And your mark on last Friday's test was better than the first one, but it was still not a pass. You're going to have to look for all the marks you can get."

Disappointed, he shuffled to his desk. On the Friday test he had actually tried to answer the questions. He scored twenty-two out of fifty. That was still not a mark he wanted to show his father. He had shoved the paper into the bottom of his backpack. This week, he would pay attention in class. That would make the difference.

Near the end of class, Ms Ramsahai walked over to Tyler's desk and slid his essay toward him, pointing to areas she had marked with grey pencil.

"You've done a good job," she said. "The research is based on your experience more than on other sources, but that's not bad for this kind of essay. Of course, it would be better to have both print references and anecdotal material, but ..." Tyler began to zone out. Teacher talk.

"What's that mean? Anek-who?" he asked. Already, his eyes had scanned ahead and he could see that she had marked several places in his essay.

"Anecdotal. A fancy word for the things that Kevin and Sam told you. And for your own experience in the race," she replied.

"Oh." Tyler's mood darkened. His throat felt tight. He had worked hard on the essay, all afternoon; it was his best writing. She hadn't even put a grade on it.

"What mark did I get?" he asked.

"I haven't graded it yet," the teacher replied. 'I've marked the places where you could fix up some spelling and punctuation. You can do that in class today. I'll mark it with the others tonight."

"No mark?"

"I'll mark the final version."

Tyler wanted to say something mean, but he held his tongue. If that was what she was going to do, then why bother? He made a fist around his pencil and jabbed it several times at the paper on his desk. The lead broke.

By dismissal time at one o'clock, Tyler had not made any corrections to his essay.

"Okay, people. Hand in your final draft. We'll see you tomorrow."

Tyler grabbed his essay, unchanged, and shuffled up to the teacher's desk. Quietly he slipped it to the bottom of the pile. He avoided Ms Ramsahai's eyes. She couldn't make him rewrite the essay.

Out the window, he could see Kevin waiting by the bicycle rack.

"Tyler!" Ms Ramsahai called as he reached the door, his backpack on by one strap. He pretended he hadn't heard. Tyler slipped quickly around the corner and out the door.

Outside, Kevin was pulling his bike from the rack and Samantha was crossing the football field.

"You up for a ride today?" he asked. "Or are you still sore from your triathlon?"

Tyler pulled an apple out of his lunch bag. "First I gotta get something to eat. If I'm going to do that triathlon in August, I have to train. That's what I learned on Saturday — if you don't train, you … strain."

Kevin laughed. "Starting out with a race is likely the hardest way to do it," he said. "You sure find out your weak spots in a hurry."

"Yeah. I found that out. I'm gonna practice getting dressed, for one thing."

"You mean the brickwork?"

"Yeah."

"Don't sweat it. Those are the things you can practice during the last week before the race when you're nervous and geared up. That's what Dad has us do."

"How is it having your dad as a coach? I mean, does he lean on you and stuff?"

"Actually, we have two coaches. Dad helps us with the running and bike training. And we have a swim coach."

"Two coaches?"

"It's three different sports, remember. Everybody's better at one part than another."

Samantha put on her bicycle helmet and snapped the fastener. "Everybody has their favourite parts. For me, they're swimming and running. Biking's the hardest."

"But you do so well at it!" Tyler exclaimed.

"Because I practice. You can get better at something even if you don't like it."

Kevin laughed. "Running's my worst part. That's why I work hardest at it. Dad says the secret is to find your weak spot."

"I found swimming tough. I was a leg behind everyone else," Tyler said.

"That's where you can improve the most. Fix up your weaknesses. I can see if our swim coach has room for one more," Kevin said. "Want me to ask?"

"That would be great!"

Later, on their bikes, Kevin led Tyler and Samantha on a ten-kilometre bike ride. Tyler noticed that Samantha could only keep up with him on the hills.

"I was bad on hills, so dad had me riding up them a lot. Now I'm not that fast on the level courses, but I can kick butt on any uphill," Samantha said after they had returned to the school.

Kevin smiled. "We're not here to beat each other up. We're here to train, not strain. That way we can help each other get better."

"Don't forget to talk to your swim coach," said Tyler.

10

The Coach

Tyler's mother called again that night. It had been almost a week since they had spoken.

"I've rearranged my vacation," she told Tyler. "You can come to Halifax as soon as you finish summer school. Then your father can come a week later, just as he planned. That'll give us a couple of weeks together. Goodness knows we need it."

"Yeah, but Mom—"

"Tyler, I know all of this has been tough on us. We'll have lots of fun …"

Tyler blew a long sigh into the telephone. "It's not that. I'd love to go. But, see, there's this triathlon. I'm running a triathlon that week. August 21."

A thousand miles away, he could hear her sigh. "Tyler, what on earth is all this lately about triathlons?"

"A race. Swimming, biking, and running. I'm training with a high-school kid. I finished fourth last weekend, so I'm going to do another one. It's …"

"Tyler, I know what a triathlon is. You're making this awfully difficult."

"Why can't you come home and watch my race? You're on vacation."

"Let me speak to your father."

"Mom, it'd—"

"Let me speak to your father. This racing. You're supposed to be catching up in English. You're not messing up your summer school, too, are you?"

Now he could actually hear anger in her voice. He had heard that from his father before. But his mother?

"I'm fine," he said, and handed the phone to his father.

* * *

Tyler spent Tuesday in class trying to ignore both Ms Ramsahai and the essay she had returned to him.

She had placed the essay face down on his desk with a firm hand just before the morning break: forty out of one hundred.

Failure.

He felt a burning lump in his throat. At one point he feared he might cry, but he rubbed his eyes hard with the back of his wrist until they hurt.

He kept glancing at Ms Ramsahai. Most of the time she had her head lowered, helping a student with work. A few times she looked up and caught his eye, so he looked away.

Finally, she came over to his desk.

"Tyler, would you like to talk about this?"

"Nothing to say," Tyler mumbled without looking up.

She pulled the desk next to his closer, and sat down sideways in the seat. "I think there is," she said. "This is all about the essay, isn't it?"

"What is?"

"Your mood. You haven't done anything today. Nor yesterday. Ever since I went over your essay. So I figured it must be about the essay."

"Duh."

"Tyler, I was proud of the way you took on this project. The job you did on the essay was great."

"Yeah, worth forty."

"It could have been worth much more. Did you go over the weaknesses I pointed out? You had a few spelling mistakes, some errors in grammar." She straightened out the crumpled essay and spread it out on the desk. "In two places you could have switched the order of paragraphs."

"So if it's so good, why'd I fail?"

Ms Ramsahai looked at Tyler. "Tyler, you can't expect to pass with twelve spelling errors and seven errors in grammar. Not in grade seven. Not in my class." She picked up Tyler's pencil and pointed at the errors she had marked.

"Big deal! Who wants to pass, anyway? Who cares?" He folded his arms.

"Tyler, the process is important. You have written what could be a great essay. I really mean that. But you seem satisfied with the mistakes, with doing less than you are capable of."

"So?"

"So this, Tyler. This essay could be worth an A. Maybe an A+. Instead, you've let these silly errors stay there. The bad mark was your choice."

"It's my business."

"Tyler, needing to improve is normal. You've got to be strong to fix things. Right now the only thing that needs fixing is your attitude. And you know what? You're the only one who can do that."

Ms Ramsahai placed the pencil back on the desk with a firm snap. It was the first time Tyler had seen her so frustrated. He looked up, startled, but said nothing.

The remaining hour of class moved slowly. Tyler eyed the clock, frequently checked the bicycle rack, and ignored Ms Ramsahai.

When the class was dismissed at one o'clock, Tyler rushed outside to meet Kevin.

"Did you see the swim coach?" he asked, impatiently.

"Yup," Kevin replied.

"Well?"

"Show up at the pool tomorrow at six-thirty in the morning. Every Monday, Wednesday, and Friday. Three days a week in the pool. And don't eat breakfast first!"

*   *   *

Tyler's father turned to him after dinner that night.

"What's this about a race in August?"

Tyler was caught by surprise. He had thought his mother decided in the end not to tell his father about the race since he hadn't mentioned it after the phone call.

"Your mother says you won't go to Halifax because of a race," he said. "What's this all about?"

Tyler faltered. He wasn't prepared for this, wasn't sure how much he could tell his father without causing problems.

"The week after summer school's out," Tyler said. "There's a triathlon at the community centre. I want to run it."

"Another one?"

"Yeah. Right here in Courtice."

"At the community centre?"

"August 21. The week after I finish summer school."

"This triathlon thing," said Mr Davidson. "I'm trying to see how it can compete with a chance to be with your mother."

"Dad, she could come home for that week just as easily as we could go out there."

"Racing in a triathlon would be a waste of time if you didn't train for it," said Mr. Davidson. "Didn't you learn that the first time? And you have too much school work to train properly."

"I've been riding my bike to school," Tyler said. "Some days I run back and forth."

"And I suppose you'd want to swim back and forth on the third day," said Mr Davidson.

"Kevin and Sam said their swim coach will coach me, too. I'm going early for that tomorrow," he said. "If I run three times a week I should be in good shape."

"You're really serious about this, aren't you?"

Tyler looked at his father. "Yes," he said.

Mr Davidson paused.

"School's first," said Mr Davidson. "Getting this summer-school credit comes first. If you don't, forget about the race. Then we'll see how it goes. I can talk to your mother about her coming here instead. I'd hoped we would get to take the ferry ride from Halifax to Dartmouth, but maybe another time. You just make sure you don't let her down."

Tyler couldn't quite make sense of that. He thought she was the one who had let him down, moving as she had. But he said nothing. He was sure he could pull off a pass in English. He would just have to do his classwork.

* * *

The next morning, Tyler awoke at five-thirty. The first thing he noticed was how loud the chorus of bird songs was in the tree outside his window. The sky had begun to glow but the sun had not yet risen. Tyler squinted and rolled out of bed. With one foot on the floor, he pulled the pillow toward his cheek.

Five more minutes, he thought, wouldn't make him late.

But in an instant he was on his feet. Five minutes' sleep might easily become two hours. He would not chance it. He went to the bathroom and slapped cold water on his face. Back in his room, he tossed his swim trunks and a towel into an old sports bag.

He rode the two-and-a-half kilometres to the school in the misty light of the early dawn. He was just locking his bike into the rack in front of the community centre when Kevin and Sam rode up.

They shivered slightly in the cool air. "Come on, let's get changed," said Kevin. "Coach will be here soon. Don't want to be late."

The change room was empty, so finding a locker was no problem.

They showered without speaking. As they headed for the pool, Kevin pulled a pair of goggles from his locker.

"You might want to get a pair of these," he said. "The chlorine might sting your eyes, but you'll be all right for today."

They emerged onto the deserted pool deck. The water was clear, without a ripple. Tyler looked up at the corkscrew slide.

"You won't get to use that slide," said Kevin. "You won't have time."

"I need to learn how to do a proper crawl," said Tyler. "You know, with your head down and breathing out the side. Isn't that's what it's called?"

"Yeah. The crawl."

"And to turn around. Some of those other swimmers hardly stop at all at the turnaround."

"Coach'll get you doing that," said Kevin. "If it's done right, the turnaround will actually speed you up. I wonder what's keeping her?"

Tyler looked at his older friend. "Her?"

"Yeah. She's good. Here she comes now."

Just then Samantha and one other swimmer emerged from

the change room. Behind them came a coach with a clipboard, a whistle around her neck, and a smile too broad for this early in the morning.

"Good morning, Tyler," she said.

It was Ms Ramsahai.

11

The Deal

Ms Ramsahai smiled and walked toward them.

"Well, Tyler," she said. "This is a surprise."

Tyler couldn't think of an answer.

"Hang on just a sec," the coach said. She blew her whistle, a small toot that got attention.

"Regular warm-up, guys," she said. "Sam, you lead. A few stretches, then four slow laps." Kevin moved to join the two girls.

Ms Ramsahai turned to Tyler.

"I'm happy to be your coach," she said, "but first we must talk."

While the other three athletes splashed and laughed through their warm-up exercises, Ms Ramsahai moved toward the sheltered area under the slide.

"We can hear a little better here," she said. "Now, first, we have to agree on what it is you're after."

Tyler swallowed, and tried to form words, but his mouth was dry.

"The triathlon. I want to do that. In August."

"That's reasonable. But what do you expect me to do for you?"

"Swimming. I need to swim better. Maybe the crawl. I dunno.

And I don't know how to turn around at the end of the pool."

"You'll likely need some endurance training," said Ms Ramsahai. "You're not used to swimming, what is it, two hundred metres?"

"A hundred and fifty."

"Six laps. We can help with that, the swimming part. But the rest: the bike, the running, the brickwork. I can't help you there."

"Kevin said he would."

Ms Ramsahai bit her lower lip. "There's one more thing," she said.

"What's that?"

"Coachability."

"Huh?"

"You mean, 'pardon.'"

"Sorry. Pardon?"

"Attitude."

Tyler looked puzzled.

"Tyler, you've been in my English class for two-and-a-half weeks. As your English coach, I'd say you haven't exactly been Olympic material."

Tyler hung his head. "I'm sorry."

"Sorry's fine, but I'm more worried about the attitude you've shown. A coach is a teacher. I can provide you with some information, point out little bits here and there, but the inspiration has to come from you. You're the one who has to do the hard work, even when you're tired and discouraged. And there will be hard work."

Tyler shuffled from foot to foot. "I know that."

"If I'm going to be your coach, I've got to be your teacher, too. For swimming and for English."

"I'll work hard."

"As your teacher I can't tell you this, but as your coach I can. So far what I've seen from you shows me you have an attitude problem. I've got to see that change. Now."

"Yes, Ms Ramsahai."

"In English class as well?"

Tyler looked at his toes. "Yes," he said.

"Show up and do the work — in the pool and in the classroom. Try your hardest and do your best. When thing get tough — dig harder. Is that a deal?" She held out her hand.

Tyler reached out and shook her hand. "Deal." He hesitated, and added, "Thanks."

"Okay, then. Jump in the pool and swim up and back so I can see what we've got to work with. We've only got four-and-a-half weeks."

* * *

That first morning Tyler worked on the crawl, swallowed water, and bumped his head three times trying to execute a flip turn at the end of the pool.

"You'll get it," said Ms Ramsahai with a laugh. "If you're tough enough to keep at it, you'll be all right."

Later, after a quick shower, Tyler, Kevin, and Samantha went to the concession stand, where Tyler bought a bagel with cream cheese for breakfast. After, they walked their bikes through the gap in the fence to the high school. Tyler still had more than a half-hour before class.

"Will Ms Ramsahai be here to let us in?" Tyler asked.

"Not for a while. She usually goes to the library after coaching," Kevin replied.

"I didn't know the library was open this early," said Tyler.

"It isn't. She has coffee with the librarian," said Kevin. "We're still riding after class today, right? It'll have to be a slow one — with this morning's swim, today is Tyler's first double workout."

"I'll be back for that," said Samantha.

"Good," said Kevin. "I'm going up to my class now. Review some stuff before class starts. See you here."

Samantha put on her bicycle helmet.

"Where do you go all morning?" Tyler asked. "You're here for swimming, and every day you're back to ride with us …"

"Hm. Library some days. Mostly, like today, I'll just go home."

"Where's that?"

"The other side of Townline Road," she said.

"Sheesh. How far is that?"

"Three kilometres. Dad measured it once. He likes to do that to keep track of how far we bike."

"Three there, three back, that's six, plus what we ride today. No wonder you're good."

"Thanks," said Samantha. "But just doing it isn't enough. You have to work on form and style, too."

She pushed away. Tyler watched her ride across the grass along the edge of the football field and cross into the school parking lot. He thought she rode with great style — even when she wasn't racing.

After she rode out of sight, Tyler sat down on the school steps and pulled his essay from the jumble of books and papers inside his backpack. He smoothed out the paper on the crumbly concrete and reread it.

Ms Ramsahai had clearly circled the mistakes, and wrote a question mark where she thought something he wrote might be in doubt. And the last two paragraphs she had wanted moved were circled.

But this time he noticed the comments he hadn't bothered

to read when she first handed the essay back to him. Now they leaped out at him. "Great research!" "That must have hurt!" "I like your writing style."

And the tiny writing at the end: "This should be a great essay. Make the changes as suggested and hand in a final copy. This should be worth a mark you'll be proud of!"

Marks or not, he knew he had a job to do. He decided to rewrite the essay.

* * *

In class the rest of that week, he was surprised at how busy he was. Before, when he hadn't bothered to do any work, he thought everyone had time, like he did, to watch the bicycle rack.

Now he found the English exercises challenging but not impossible. Every time his mind started to stray, he looked up at Ms Ramsahai and quickly returned to work.

On Thursday morning, he entered the class several minutes before the rest of the students. Ms Ramsahai was busy writing at her desk.

"I've rewrote my essay," he said, placing it on her desk.

"Rewritten, Tyler," said Ms Ramsahai with a smile.

"Rewritten," he repeated.

"Well, let's see what you've got." She glanced at the paper and looked up. "Tyler, this has already been marked. It—"

"I know, but I just wanted you to have a look at it, to see if I did what you had asked, to see if I did it right." He almost said, "If I hadn't been such a jerk," but he didn't. "So that I'll know if I'm on the right track. So that next time I'll get it right."

"I'll get it back to you as soon as I can."

On Friday in the pool, he started to work on his crawl stroke. Sam helped him.

"You're veering out of your lane," Ms Ramsahai called. "You keep breathing on the right side, and it pulls you in that direction. You'll end up getting disqualified."

"I'll straighten it up."

"We don't have enough time. Besides, when you get into a race, you'll be tuckered out, on those last two laps especially. That's when you'll start going out of your lane. Try breathing with every stroke; left, right, left, right. There, that's it. You've got the stroke down quite well. Next week we'll see if you can learn to breathe."

"Great."

"Think you can hold your breath until then?" asked Samantha grinning.

In class that day, Ms Ramsahai returned his triathlon essay. A new mark was written boldly on the title page: eighty-three out of one hundred!

"You did a very good job with this," she said, "so I decided to accept your revised essay. This mark will count. Keep it up and you'll end up with a mark to be proud of. You have only two bad test scores to overcome, but those were the first two weekly tests, and don't count for much of the final mark."

"You mean I might pass?" asked Tyler.

"Well, this essay is a good sign. Want to see how you did on today's Friday test?"

She plunked the paper face down on his desk and held it there.

Tyler had hoped his new tactic of paying attention in class would pay off. A couple of questions on this test had relied on information from the first two weeks, though, and he knew he had missed those.

"Now, what are you going to do with the questions you didn't get right?"

Tyler shook his head at the unexpected question.

"Review them," he said, finally, rolling his eyes.

"Right answer. Good attitude."

Slowly, she turned the paper over.

Tyler's mouth fell open. It said thirty-four out of fifty. He had passed.

"Not brilliant, but it's a start," the teacher said.

12

Found Out

Two weeks later, Tyler finally got an A on his weekly test. He called his mother in Halifax to tell her.

"An A!" he said loudly, so his father could hear from the patio, where he was barbecuing hamburgers.

"Well, that's great," she said. "What did your father say?"

"He says it's great. And ..." He lifted the mouthpiece away from his face and raised his voice, again for his father's benefit, "I got an A on my triathlon essay, too!" He put the phone back to his ear. "I didn't want to tell anybody until I got another one to go with it."

"Your dad says your training is going well, too."

"I'm still working on my somersault turn, and if I try to speed up, my breathing gets out of whack."

"You'll get it. You don't seem so angry any more."

"Are you still going to be able to make it up for my race?" Tyler asked.

"I'll be there. That's what, two weeks? How time flies! If I get on the train Thursday at midnight I'll be there Friday by four-thirty or so."

Tyler's father came into the kitchen, brandishing his spatula. He wore an apron that said *Chief Beef*. Tyler thought it looked stupid.

"Dad wants to talk to you."

His father looked up and smiled.

"Oh, Tyler, I'm sorry you had to go to summer school," his mother said. "I've been thinking … if I'd been home this year, I would have been able to help you keep your marks up. I'm glad you're doing well."

"It's okay. I've got a great teacher. She says I would have to work hard to fail now; blow the final test completely or something. She also says I could still get an A on the whole course."

"That's good news, Tyler."

"Where do you keep your tests?" Tyler's father said, peering out into the hallway. Tyler's backpack lay in the front hall.

"You're lucky to have a good teacher," said Mrs Davidson on the phone.

"They in your backpack?" his father asked from the front hall. "The tests? I'd like to see them."

Tyler nodded to his father. His mother continued on the phone. "I suppose I could get away a day early, maybe by early Thursday evening. We'll see how things go at work. We all have so much to talk about. This is no way to be a family, this far apart. I miss you so much."

"Mom?"

"Yes, Tyler?"

In the hall, his father rummaged through the backpack. "Is there anything you don't keep in here?" he asked, lifting out two text books, a dictionary, a notebook, and a handful of papers.

"Mom, are you really coming back in a year?"

There was silence from the other end of the phone. In the hall, Tyler could see his father, still bent over the backpack. His face was turning red.

"Mom?"

"Tyler, we keep telling you this is only temporary. Your father and I are not planning to get divorced. All that's happened right now is that our jobs are a thousand miles apart. But …"

"It's my family, too."

"… I know that, Tyler. I'm not saying this is easy for any of us."

"But you can't be my mom if you're living in Halifax."

"Tyler, I'll always be your mom."

"That's what Diggy Rodriguez's father said before he moved to Vancouver."

"Tyler, my job got moved. It happens. And this is only a short-term contract."

Tyler's father came back into the room, sorting through the loose papers he had pulled from the backpack. He exhaled slowly.

"Well?" Mrs Davidson asked.

Tyler didn't answer.

"It was also an opportunity to gain some experience in graphics, which I would never get to do otherwise. You're not the only one who learns things, son."

"Yeah, but …"

"Tyler, that's all that happened. And your father and I discussed it. Loudly. That's all."

She paused. "Can I talk to your father now?"

Tyler's father turned slowly, his eyes wide. He held out an almost blank sheet of paper.

"What's this?" he demanded, holding the paper out toward Tyler.

"It's …" Tyler swallowed hard. It was his first English test. He could read Ms Ramsahai's mark in the top left corner: zero.

"Dad, it's not what you think."

"And this?" said his father, holding up a second paper. Twenty-three out of fifty. The second test.

"These don't look like A's to me," his father said. He thrust the papers toward Tyler with one hand and grabbed the phone with the other.

"Elizabeth, it's Charlie. I'll call you back. And you don't need to worry about that race. Tyler won't be running it. He's been lying to us. I'll tell you about it later." He hung up the phone and turned on Tyler.

"I want an explanation," he said, trembling with anger. He grabbed the papers back.

"Zero." He said, holding up the first test in one hand, then thrusting the second test forward with the other. "And twenty-three."

Tyler burbled, "But, I ..." But he could think of nothing to say.

"They don't look like good marks to me."

Finally, Tyler recovered his voice. "Those were the first two marks. I wasn't trying then. I can show you the other marks ..."

Tyler reached out for the binder with the latest tests. He had carefully snapped each into place, filing them in the back. He had been so thrilled that afternoon.

"You lied!" his father said, close to shouting now. "You lied to me. You're grounded. Flat. No race. Nothing."

"I didn't lie! I didn't!"

"You misled me! That's just as bad! You had these marks and you didn't tell me! Now go to your room and get to work."

Tyler's father still held the spatula in a trembling hand.

"To your room," he repeated.

Outside, a billow of smoke from the burned hamburgers clouded the kitchen window.

13

Giving Up

At school the following Monday, Ms Ramsahai kept looking down the row of empty desks at Tyler. He avoided her gaze. He crossed his arms and slumped in his seat. All morning he had ignored his classwork.

Before the morning break, Ms Ramsahai put down her chalk and moved toward the classroom door.

"Fifteen minutes, everybody," she said. Tyler rose to go, to be first out the door, but Ms Ramsahai blocked his way. He dropped back into his seat.

"I want to talk to you," she said. Tyler watched as his classmates filed out.

"Yeah," Tyler said, meeting her gaze.

"Tyler, you weren't at swim practice this morning," she said.

"Nope," Tyler snorted. After being grounded, why bother, he thought. His father wouldn't have allowed it anyway. His anger surged, his throat burned.

"Do you want to explain that to me?"

Ms Ramsahai's expression surprised him: she looked hurt. Tyler's anger had actually caused pain to an adult. The discovery astounded him.

"I quit." He stood up, He was surprised to realize he was taller than his teacher. He knew he was really angry with his father. But he had been seething all weekend. Any adult was fair game.

"I quit," he repeated, spitting the words. He slipped sideways past the teacher and out the classroom door.

His classmates had gone to the cafeteria to buy chocolate bars and pop from the vending machines. He didn't talk much to them, anyway. Why would they care?

He kicked the release bar to open the outside door. To the south, toward Lake Ontario, huge black thunder clouds rumbled. Tyler stood by the bicycle rack and thought about going for a ride. A *long* ride. That would serve them right, he thought.

Samantha was crossing the football field toward him.

"You missed swim class this morning," she said as she approached, her usual smile replaced with a slight frown. "Ms Ramsahai was worried."

"I can't come again," he said. "Ever."

"Why? Something happen?"

Tyler couldn't find words. His anger was harder to maintain with Samantha. "I've … I've been … grounded."

"Grounded? Why?"

Now that it was out, he wanted to talk about it. To share the unfairness.

"My dad found two tests I failed, and went into shock. Accused me of lying and cheating."

"But you've been doing so well!"

"He didn't want to listen. Said I lied. So I'm grounded even longer than before. Can't come to swim practice. Can't go riding or running. Can't even go in the race."

Samantha picked up Tyler's bicycle helmet from where it hung from his handlebars and ran one finger around the rim.

"Are you still going to ride this afternoon?" she asked.

"Can't. My father says I have to be home by one-thirty. Or

else." He didn't know what his father's "or else" meant. Maybe he would ride anyway, just to find out.

"What did Ms Ramsahai say?" Samantha asked.

"Why would she care? She just wants to trick me into doing school work. Well, it won't work. I quit everything." Tyler spat out the last words.

"Tyler, Ms Ramsahai isn't like that. She's a good coach."

"Yeah, right."

A cooling breeze from the coming storm turned the leaves of nearby maples inside out. Out over the lake, a shaft of lightning jumped from cloud to cloud, followed by a rumble of thunder. One solitary raindrop felt cold on Tyler's cheek.

"Ms Ramsahai is a good coach," Samantha repeated, as Tyler turned to enter the school. "She is, she really is. She cares about you."

Tyler felt himself sliding into a hole. He didn't want anyone to care about him.

*　*　*

Tyler's father was still angry on Tuesday afternoon. He gripped the car's steering wheel as though it were a hockey stick. Tyler could see his jaw working back and forth as he ground his teeth. He could *hear* his father grinding his teeth.

"Tell me what this is about," Mr Davidson said, unclenching his teeth just enough to hiss the words. "If this is another of your surprises, you'd better tell me now."

The truth was, Tyler didn't know what anything was about anymore. Ms Ramsahai had called his father. That's all he knew.

"I can only tell you that I don't like getting calls from teachers," Mr Davidson said. "I don't like having to clean up after you, young man."

Tyler slumped further down in his seat.

"You'll strangle yourself on the seatbelt sitting like that," said his father. Tyler shifted, but remained hunched over.

The night before, his parents had fought again on the phone. He hoped his mother had taken his side about the race, but the frustrating thing was that he didn't know. But they had fought, he could hear it in his room. Not the details, just the rumble of his father's deep voice and the slamming down of the receiver.

As they arrived at the school, Mr Davidson pulled sharply into the parking lot and jammed the van into the parking spot nearest to the main entrance. Tyler was pushed forward in his seat.

"One last chance to fill me in before we go in there," his father said. "One last chance."

Tyler said nothing. He opened the door and slid out.

Tyler slouched along behind his father through the halls to the English classroom.

"It wouldn't hurt you to move a bit," his father said gruffly.

Tyler didn't answer. He just glared at his father and continued his insolent shuffle.

At the classroom door, his father stopped and turned. "One last time," he said. "What's this about? I've told you I don't like surprises. Well, this better not be one."

14

The Teacher

Ms Ramsahai sat upright at the teacher's desk at the rear of the room, her elbows propped on the desk.

"Thank you for coming," she said, rising, as Tyler followed his father into the classroom. She shook hands with Mr Davidson and pointed to two chairs that had been pulled up in front, facing the desk. "Have a seat."

"Miss Ranshani, I want to know what Tyler's ..." His father started out in a bluster.

"Ms Ramsahai," corrected the teacher.

"Ms Ramsahai, sorry." Tyler's father lowered himself slowly into the too-small chair.

"What's this about?" he said, finally.

"Two things: this English class, and swimming lessons. Mr Davidson, did you know that Tyler has been taking swimming lessons from me three mornings a week for the past three weeks?"

"From you?"

"Swimming lessons. Six-thirty every morning, for two hours."

"He told me about the lessons. I didn't know you were coaching."

Tyler felt his father's eyes descend on him, but he dared not look back.

"First lying to me about your tests," he said to Tyler. "And now this. What else are you hiding?" He turned back to Ms Ramsahai. "We will pay for swimming lessons."

"Paying for the lessons is not a big deal," Ms Ramsahai said. "What the lessons mean to Tyler is."

"His priority is to pass his lessons in his summer-school course."

"Of course it is. Mr Davidson, I can't tell you how to run your family. I can only present you with the viewpoint of a teacher and a coach. Did you know that your son wants to run a triathlon a week from Saturday?"

Tyler's father nodded. "He told me about that. And I was willing to allow that — as long as he kept his grades up. But that's not possible now."

"Are you sure?"

"I've seen his tests."

"Yes, but you may not have seen all of his tests. Do you think participation in sports is important?"

"Not as important as passing an English course. And he lied to me."

"It may seem that way."

"He isn't going to pass English by getting goose eggs on tests," Mr Davidson replied. "It's bad enough he failed a grade-seven English class once. I'll do anything I can to make sure it doesn't happen again."

Ms Ramsahai leaned forward in her chair. "Tyler did not 'fail,' as you put it. He was recommended for remedial work. And do you mean that?" she asked.

"Mean what?"

"That you'd do anything to make sure he gets the skills he needs at school?"

"Of course I do. What do you think this is all about?"

Ms Ramsahai leaned further forward, her forearms splayed across the desk. Still locking eyes with Mr Davidson, she said: "Tyler, you heard how determined your father is. He'll do anything to get you to pass this course."

Tyler nodded, not sure where the conversation was going.

"Anything?" the teacher repeated.

"Anything," Tyler's father responded.

Ms Ramsahai turned to Tyler. "Tyler, you've said that you want to run this triathlon a week from Saturday."

Tyler nodded, still baffled.

"What would you do to make sure you run that race, Tyler?"

Tyler looked at his teacher, then at his father. The papers on Ms Ramsahai's desk were lined up neatly, precisely, as though this had all been carefully laid out. Tyler shifted in the uncomfortable chair.

"What would you sacrifice for this, Tyler?"

Tyler hesitated.

"Anything," he replied.

Ms Ramsahai smiled. "So you each know what you want. Perhaps you can work things out so you both win." She rearranged the papers on her desk. "There are some things here I want to show you, Mr Davidson."

Tyler watched as she spread out three piles of papers and reversed them so his father could read them.

"These are copies of Tyler's last three tests. Did he show them to you?"

"He said … yes, I saw those. I also saw two tests that he failed. That was enough for me."

"These are his latest results. Those first two tests count very little toward the final mark. These later tests are weighted more heavily. Can you see the trend?"

Tyler's father leaned forward. Ms Ramsahai reached out and

on each paper carefully circled in red the mark: C, B, A.

"It …" Mr Davidson's mouth worked but no sound came.

"Tyler is well on the way to acing this course."

"He … he … lied."

"Mr Davidson, I'm a teacher and a coach. I can point out what needs to be done, but it's the swimmer who has to do the swimming. Same in English. The student has to do the learning."

"Tyler lied to me," Mr Davidson repeated.

"If he did, that is wrong. But at this stage, you should be looking at the big picture. Both of you. Mr Davidson, you said you'd do anything to get Tyler to pass this course. Tyler, you said you'd do anything to get a chance to run in the triathlon. That sounds like a win-win to me. You two just need to work out the details."

She rose and shook hands with Tyler's father, then turned to Tyler and offered her hand to him.

"There are three more days of class left before the final test. There's nothing more I can do. I suggest you go home and discuss how you can both achieve your goals. Before the clock runs out."

* * *

The drive home was silent. Tyler watched out of the corner of his eye as his father slouched against the driver's side door. He held the steering wheel with one hand, and ran his fingers through his hair with the other.

After Mr Davidson pulled the van into their driveway, Tyler jumped out and headed for the front door.

"Show me your bike," his father said, moving slowly from the vehicle.

"Bike?" repeated Tyler, knowing it sounded dumb.

"Bike. In the garage."

Still puzzled, Tyler unlatched the garage door and rolled it up. The garage was filled with junk: cardboard boxes, uncollected newspapers, two old rocking chairs, a desk, and three garbage bags of empty pop cans that had missed the recycling pick-up three times.

Tyler's bicycle rested against the box that held their Christmas tree. He pulled it out into the sunshine, picked it up, and turned to face his father, dropping the bike so it bounced on its tires between them.

"There."

His father looked at the bike, gripped the crossbar, and shook the frame. "That strong enough?" he asked. "When I was a kid they used to make girls' bikes without the crossbar so it wouldn't get in the way of skirts. Do they do that any more?"

"No, Dad. Sam ..."

"Does this thing have enough speeds for you to race with?" his father continued.

Tyler nodded. "I've been using it to train," he said. "Kevin says he'll loan me his old bike for the race."

"Kevin?" Tyler knew then that he and his father had a lot of catching up to do.

"He's the guy I went to the race in Lindsay with. He's training for the triathlon. Him and his sister, Sam. Samantha."

Mr Davidson picked the bike up by the seat and handlebars, dropped it from ten centimetres, and watched it bounce, as Tyler had done.

"It's a cross-country bike," he said at last. "Pretty heavy. This Kevin guy: his old bike work okay?"

"He trains on it. Yeah, it's pretty good. His father bought him a new one for racing."

His father grinned. "Well, don't be expecting that for a while," he said. "This father doesn't quite have money like that. Just because you're going to run one race doesn't mean …"

"You mean I can go in the race?" Tyler asked. "Really?"

"Ah-ah-ah. Not too hasty. Yes. But there are … conditions."

"Anything."

"You've said that. You must pass your English course."

"Done."

"You must train properly from now until then."

"You mean swim classes, too?"

"Swim classes, too."

"Done."

Mr Davidson pulled down the garage door. "You go back to training," he said. "As Ms Ramsahai pointed out, your marks started improving when you started training for this. So you get back to training. *And* do your homework." He placed one hand on Tyler's shoulder.

"Just do your best," he said. "Even when we run into rough patches, we have to try our hardest. Especially at these times."

Tyler blinked once in the August sunshine. "Thanks, Dad," he said.

"And one more condition."

Tyler looked at his father.

"Phone your mother. Now."

15

Sam's Fuss

A week later, Sam caught up to him at the bicycle rack after swim class.

"Something's still not right," she said.

Tyler looked at her, puzzled. Since his father had relented, the swim lessons had resumed. He had worked hard, and he could feel himself getting better.

"With what? You?"

Sam shook out her helmet. "No, silly. With you. Did everything finish up all right in English class? Kevin passed his math final. He was *so* glad. But you. Something's still bothering you."

"I passed. I even scored an A on the last test. I ended up with B+ on the whole course. My dad was really happy."

Sam looked at him with her clear blue eyes. As always, he was always the first to look away. "Let's go get a bottle of pop," she said.

Now that summer school was over, the whole day was theirs. With three days left before the triathlon, their training had been cut back.

They bought drinks at the corner store, walked their bikes back to the community centre, and found some shade in the woods behind the high school.

"You still mad at your mom?" Sam asked.

Tyler shrugged. "She's coming for the race. Maybe staying for a few days. Said she has a week's holiday."

"I asked if you were still mad at her."

"I dunno. I guess. How would you feel if your mom left?"

Sam slurped with her straw from the bottom of the can. "My mom did leave."

Tyler looked at her. "I didn't know," he said. "I'm sorry."

"Don't be. It was two years ago. She left, then she came back, and then Dad left."

"But I thought …"

"We both live with our mother now. We see Dad on weekends, for training sessions, and sometimes for movies. He's around a lot. And now they talk. They're divorced, but they're both still really nice people."

Tyler picked up a stick and he stuck it in the ground again and again, flicking dirt with each jab.

"So what are you saying?"

"I don't know. That they're nice people, my parents. Why are you mad at her? Them?"

"I'm not."

"Yeah, but you've been pretty hard on her."

"You mean like when I didn't talk to her for three months? That's in the past. I talked to her the night before last."

"So she's happy, you're happy, and your dad's happy. But your mom's going back to Halifax next week. Why's that?"

"Because. She says this job lets her do things she hasn't done before."

Sam dropped her pop bottle in a garbage can. "Think that's true?" she asked. "Or is it just an excuse?"

Tyler thought for a moment. "Even before her job moved, she did a lot of work at home. I didn't see why she couldn't still do that."

"So you hassled her?"

Tyler shrugged. "I was ticked," he said.

Sam looked him straight in the eye. "Look, Tyler. If your dad had taken a job in Halifax, what do you suppose would have happened?"

"I dunno. We would have moved there, likely. Why?"

"And when your mother gets a chance to do the same thing?"

"But that's not the same!"

Sam put her hands on both of his shoulders and gently pushed him away. "What's not the same? Tyler, is there any reason it can't be equal? Why should the father move and take the family but not the mother?"

Tyler swallowed, surprised. "Because ... because it's a one-year job!" he said. "No use moving out there for a one-year job."

"And if your father had a one-year job? Then it'd be okay for him to go away like that?"

"That would be different."

"Oh? How would that be different? Because you'd be living back home with your mother? Sounds like two sets of rules to me!"

Tyler backed along the path. "They fought. Then they said they wouldn't get divorced."

"Well, it doesn't seem like they are. It sounds more like you just didn't believe them."

"They said it was for me, so I didn't have to change schools."

Sam began walking, fast, back to their bicycles. "Then there was no use making such a fuss," she said. "Everybody works so hard to help you, Tyler. Your father, Ms Ramsahai, Kevin, even my father. Your mother, too. But sometimes you are a self-centred brat with a bad attitude who doesn't deserve it. Have you ever thought that maybe it's time you helped your mother out on this one?"

"Help her?" Tyler asked.

"Tell her it's okay. She probably feels like crap because of the way you been acting. You've got your way this time. Maybe you should give a little."

16

The Return

Tyler's mother stepped off the train carrying three pieces of luggage. She smiled broadly when she saw Tyler on the platform.

"Tyler!" she cried, hugging him tightly. Tyler welcomed her embrace, even though they were in public.

Mrs Davidson was dressed in jeans, thick-soled shoes, a light top, and a wide-brimmed hat. She grabbed Tyler's hand with one hand, wrapped her other around her husband's waist, and pulled them both toward the parking lot.

"I've missed you two!" she said.

Tyler asked, turning to his mother. "Can you stay the whole week?"

She laughed. "Things got messy at work, but I've got a week. We all still have so much to talk about." She stood on her tip-toes and kissed her husband on the cheek.

"I'll get the luggage," Mr Davidson said, returning the kiss and putting one hand on Tyler's shoulder.

Mrs Davidson spun around once, her arms outstretched. "It's so good to be home!" she said, then gripped Tyler's hand and took on a more serious look.

"I'm not sure what made the difference. Do you remember when I was first offered this job last Christmas? And how your father didn't like the idea?"

"He wasn't the only one."

"Well, I love the job, but not the location."

"I thought you love Halifax."

"I do, but it's too far away from you two."

"I thought you were going to get divorced. Then you left."

"It was painful for all of us," his mother replied, bitting her lower lip. "Yes, we fought. Not with each other so much as with the choices we had to make. I just wish you didn't have to go through all of this."

"I've been a pain. I'm sorry for all that stuff."

Tyler's mother pulled him forward into a hug. "We've always wanted to be together. Always. Your father was willing to move to Halifax and work with his clients by e-mail and phone. But there was no way I was going to move you out across the country to start the eighth grade. Not for a one-year contract."

"Don't you think that would be partly my choice?"

Tyler's father came back, lugging his mother's two large suitcases. "You bring a brick collection?" he asked. "Or are you an anvil saleslady?"

"Dad, you promised — no more lame jokes."

"I couldn't resist. I heard you two talking. But one day we were struggling to make the right choice, and the next we seemed to fighting over who was going to win: your mother or me. None of this has been fair to you."

"But it wouldn't have been fair for Mom not to take that job!" Tyler blurted.

"Or for you to switch schools," said his father.

"It's not a matter of either my job here or your mother's job in Halifax," said his father. "It's a matter of how we make this family work. It means compromise."

Tyler's mother brushed his cheek.

"You mean we just have to make this work so that everybody wins," said Tyler.

"And we have a big decision to make. We can talk about it all week."

"What do you mean?"

"It's my job," said Tyler's mother. "They've offered to make it permanent."

"In Halifax?"

"In Halifax. So it seems we need to talk about this and make a decision."

"I've already made mine," said Tyler.

"Well, we don't need to deal with that until next week, when we'll have lots of time. Now, young man, tell me about this race of yours tomorrow."

"First he'll show you his report from his English course," said Mr Davidson. "Amazing what this kid can do when he puts his mind to it."

17

Race Day

When Tyler arrived at the community centre at eight o'clock on the morning of the race, crowds had already begun to gather.

Part of the parking lot had been roped off for the transition area from the pool to the bike. Course marshals, donning brightly coloured safety vests, emerged three at a time from the community centre.

Tyler met Kevin at the corner by the library.

"I'm glad I picked up my registration pack yesterday," he said. "Getting crowded already."

Kevin pointed to his father's SUV with their three bikes mounted upside-down on the roof rack. "We better get the bikes now," he said. "Dad wants to park over at the school so he can get out."

With some help from Kevin's father, they unstrapped the bicycles and walked them over to the transition area. The bicycle racks had been set up in parallel rows, with three metres between each one. The racks were numbered so that each of the 275 competitors had their own spot.

"I'm glad we did the brickwork this week," said Tyler. "I can't believe how much time I lost in Lindsay."

Kevin shrugged. "Everybody does in their first race. It's a learning experience."

Sam came up behind him. "Your folks here yet?"

Tyler smiled. "Mom came in from Halifax yesterday." He glanced around. "They're coming down later for the start of my race. We might be moving to Halifax, actually."

"You okay with that?" she asked.

"It's going to be a family decision this time," he said.

"We'll be cheering for you off the start," Sam said. "We'll make some noise. Then I'll be off to start my heat."

"I'll cheer you across the finish line," Tyler said. "Have a great race!"

In the brilliant sunshine, the parking lot had taken on a carnival-like feel. Parents helped racers set up bikes, clothes, shoes, and towels in the transition area. A long line of small, hat-like orange traffic cones lined the long lane leading to Courtice Road.

Out near the road, marshals were already in place. A hundred metres away, at Nash Road, a police car sat with its lights flashing while a police officer directed traffic.

All of a sudden the whole scene — the lane, the roadway, the adjacent football field at the high school, the parking lot, the transition area — changed tone. Traffic on the road had been stopped. The crowd buzzed with a quiet anticipation.

* * *

Tyler shivered on the apron of the swimming pool while lining up for his race. In the pool, younger racers splashed through the pool leg of their triathlon. Tyler stood with his back against the wall, waiting.

His legs quivered. His teeth chattered. He windmilled his arms forward, then back, and felt a mild warmth as his muscles loosened up.

Eventually, the last of the younger racers left the pool. Ms

Ramsahai waved through the glass wall in front of the spectator area until he looked up, smiled, and gave a little wave back. The room fell silent and the pool, moments before churned by swimmers, calmed. Tyler could hear only the slap-slap of water on the pool's edge.

"Boys twelve to thirteen, Heat One!" barked an official, raising her arm.

Tyler moved to the edge of the pool.

The official held her arm aloft, a walkie-talkie pressed to her ear.

"Ready!"

Tyler tensed, arms behind him, and curled his toes for a better grip.

All breathing stopped.

A whistle blast pierced the air. Before the first echo sounded, Tyler was gone, launching through the air and slicing into the water like a torpedo. He came up three metres out, churning.

His mornings of pool training took over. Like paddlewheels, his arms circled up and over: stroke, breathe, stroke, breathe. His nervous energy now fuelled him.

Control, he thought; control. He fought the urge to sprint ahead, to take the lead. Even so, as he somersaulted into the turnaround he saw that he was even with the leaders.

Stroke, breathe, stroke, breathe. "Keep up the rhythm," Ms Ramsahai had said.

He dipped into the second turnaround; two laps gone, four to go. Third place, a length behind the leader. His pool plan had been simple — not to be last. He pulled each stroke evenly, hands cupped, elbows up and bent on the upstroke, just as Ms Ramsahai had said.

At the third turn, Tyler thrust off the end of the pool a mere two body lengths behind the leader. Without warning, his arms grew weights.

Oxygen debt.

Despite his training, despite his work, the excitement of the start had hurled him into a pace he could not keep up. The early speed had used up oxygen faster than he could replace it.

Ms Ramsahai had warned them, had even given them training drills designed to purposely put them into oxygen debt so they could recognize the signs.

"Don't panic. Keep the rhythm. Stroke! Stroke!"

He could hear her voice now. He pressed on. He increased his effort and felt his speed slow. By the fourth turn — only two laps to go — the leaders had pulled away.

He kicked off the end of the pool, torpedoed ahead, and picked up his rhythm: arm over arm, breathe, stroke, stroke.

At the hatch line marking the last turnaround, he dipped into a final somersault, flipping underwater as he had been taught. He kicked against the end of the pool, trying once again to pick up his pace.

He came out of the pool fifth — not the last of the six competitors. A towel was thrust toward him.

He stumbled along the ribbon of carpet, his feet slapping, water dripping from his bathing suit.

In the transition area, he pulled running shorts over his swimsuit, wrestled into a T-shirt, and sat on the pavement next to his bike. He carefully dried his feet with the towel. The socks gave him the most trouble. His shoes slipped on easily, though, and he tightened the laces and double knotted them. A loose lace later would cost him more time; a lace in the sprocket could keep him from finishing, or even lead to serious injury.

Finally, his helmet snapped into place.

He grabbed his bike by the handlebars and looked down the

lane to the road. Two leaders had already left, and two racers were on their way out. One other struggled with his shoes.

Quickly, Tyler pushed the bike through the funnel of cones. At the starting line, he placed one foot on the pedal and lifted himself onto the seat.

"Attaboy, Tyler!" yelled his father from amid the throng lining the long laneway to the road.

"Go, Tyler, go!" yelled his mother from beside his father. His parents were jumping up and down in unison.

Wobbly on the bike, Tyler reached down for the pedals. His legs felt frozen. He had left the bike in top gear. When he reached to gear down, the rider who was putting on his shoes earlier zipped by him.

Clunk! The gear fell into place. Immediately the pedals responded. He rose from the seat, pumping hard, steady, eager to build the speed needed to catch to the racers ahead of him. He pulled even with the bike ahead — last place.

He took the turn onto Courtice Road on the inside, pulling slightly ahead of the racer at his side as he did. On the uphill toward the tennis courts, he edged ahead by a length.

At Nash Road, where the police car blocked traffic, a white-haired race marshal wearing an orange safety vest and holding a walkie-talkie directed the racers.

"Bikes to the inside, runners on the outside," he barked. Bikers and runners shared this part of the course.

Around the corner, the road dipped. Tyler picked up speed and slammed into a higher gear. He lowered his head and settled into an even, strong pace.

Fifth place. At least not last — but the last rider panted along behind him close enough to hear.

Traffic cones divided the road. Runners and bikers, their faces flushed, flailed away on either side. Suddenly he was past the one-kilometre mark and the runners were gone, their turn-around point past.

He had ridden this section of Nash Road many times before with Kevin and Samantha, and he knew every bump. He pushed harder. For once he could ignore the stop signs.

Ahead, two riders were exchanging the lead so they could draft off of one another in an attempt to catch the leaders. At Solina Road, he pulled in behind them.

He worked his way through the small pack, twice taking his turn in the lead. But the third time he dug harder, opening up a gap that the others couldn't match. Third place!

Surging down the steep hill before Maple Grove Road, Tyler pushed into high gear and took aim at the backs of the two riders still ahead.

At the turnaround — a traffic cone in the middle of the road — Tyler gained on the second rider. He rose on his toes and pressed hard.

The road levelled, and he could see he was gaining. But what had been a sharp downhill became a very steep uphill after Maple Grove Road. Tyler clunked into a lower gear, then lower again, trying to hold his cadence for as long as possible.

Tyler remembered Trull's Road Mountain and slammed now into the lowest gear, stood on his pedals, and ground his way, stroke by stroke, up the hill.

But his hard-won gains from the turnaround had disappeared. By the time he crested the hill, the first and second racers had pulled about three hundred metres ahead.

He put his head down and drove his legs into a steady rhythm.

At least, he told himself, I won't finish last. He didn't dare look back.

18

Big Finish

Tyler grimaced as he approached the police car with its still-flashing lights at Courtice Road.

He stood on the pedals. The marshal waved him to the outside, closest to the police car.

"Runners on the inside, bicycles on the outside," bellowed the white-haired man.

Tyler turned south on Courtice Road and passed by the tennis courts onto a steep downhill. He picked up his cadence and clicked into a higher gear. Already, the second-place rider had turned into the community centre two hundred metres ahead. The leader has now nearing the transition area in the parking lot.

Tyler lowered his head and gained more speed. At the turn into the community centre, he braked only slightly, taking the corner wide and too fast. At the last moment, he tightened the turn, his front wheel glancing off the curb. Now he had a straight run into the transition area.

The crowd was strung out along the sidewalk, cheering and jumping, encouraging every competitor. He could see his parents again, still close together.

Kevin waved frantically and pointed.

"Go, go, go!" he yelled.

Tyler dismounted and trotted to his bike rack. The two leaders had already racked their bikes, secured their helmets to them, and were headed back out for the two-kilometre run.

Tyler thrust his bike into the rack and fastened his helmet to the handlebars.

"Third!" Kevin yelled "Go get the leader, man! Go get 'im. Go get 'im!"

On his feet now, Tyler wobbled out the long laneway from the community centre. His legs, still tight from biking, would not allow him to find a rhythm.

After 100 metres, though, his legs had lost their wobble. He turned uphill onto Courtice Road with a slightly shortened stride.

When he made the right turn at the tennis courts, he noticed that he had shortened the gap to the next runner.

He swept by the marshal, lengthened his stride, and quietly closed the gap even more. Then, he boldly surged, pulling ahead by one, then two strides. Just then, a bicycle rider on the same course slipped in beside him.

"Lookin' good," said Sam, for a moment pacing him before she zoomed ahead to catch the leader in her heat. "Keep it going."

Second place!

An orange pylon marked the turnaround. Ahead, the leader swivelled left around it.

Tyler counted strides: … eighteen, nineteen, twenty, then he, too, made the turn. He focused his eyes on the back of the leader's shirt.

The level course turned uphill again for 200 metres before returning to Courtice Road. Tyler shortened his stride and worked his arms: pump, kick, pump, kick.

The August sun beat down on the top of his head. Fatigue gripped him.

At the tennis court turn he rose on the balls of his feet for the downhill, finding fresh energy when he caught sight of the finish line. Three hundred more metres!

He could now see only the leader's back. Stride by stride, he pulled it nearer to him. He drank in the air, all of his muscles screaming. At the final turn, the marshal beckoned in slow motion, waving on the leader and then Tyler in for the final sprint.

Now he could see the tape at the finish line. To his right, a wall of people waved, shouted, jumped, and screamed. A wave of sound lifted him; time seemed to freeze. With fifty metres left he pulled even with the leader, matched his grunting breath, and slapped his shoes in a matching stride on the hot August pavement. From the corner of one eye he could see his parents waving their arms. His mother bounced twice, three times on the spot, in slow motion, then turned and hugged his father.

In an instant Tyler was past them, matching the leader stride for stride, each step a joy, each stride an effort.

"Now!" yelled Kevin. "Take him. Now!"

With his last ounce of energy, he lunged ahead, a centimetre, ten, a hundred, half a metre, crossing the line a full stride ahead. He had won his heat.

* * *

"Way to go, man!" said Kevin who greeted him with a high five.

Tyler bent over, gasping for air. The second-place finisher, his hands on his hips, gasping for air, reached out a hand.

"Great run, guy!" he said, offering a forearm grip.

"You, too," Tyler replied. "You, too."

Tyler's parents appeared out of the crowd.

"You won your heat!" said his father. "Wow! Next year you're going to be racing for the top! That was fantastic." He seemed to be unable to decide between a handshake and a hug, finally settling for an awkward half of each.

His mother had no such problem. She reached through the crowd and hugged her sweating son tightly.

"I'm so proud!" she said.

As Tyler introduced Kevin, Ms Ramsahai joined them.

"And this is my swim coach," Tyler said.

"And English teacher!" added his father.

"Ms Ramsahai, this is my mom!"

"That was quite a finish," Ms Ramsahai said. "Congratulations!"

"Well, thanks to you I didn't drown," Tyler said.

"Thanks to Ms Ramsahai you aren't still doing English homework!" said Tyler's father. Everyone laughed.

Ms Ramsahai turned to Kevin. "Good luck," she said. "We'll be watching."

"Watching?" said Tyler. "We'll be cheering loudly. Good luck, Kev."

Tyler's father reached out to shake Ms Ramsahai's hand. "We all want to thank you for what you've done," he said. "It has meant more than you can imagine."

Ms Ramsahai shook hands with both of Tyler's parents. "It has been a delight to have Tyler in my English class," she said. "And to coach him, too."

Tyler stood with his parents. He looked at his teacher and coach.

"Thanks," he said with a smile. "You know, summer school really wasn't my choice. But it turned out to be a pretty good way to spend a summer."

"It must have been my essays that did it," laughed Ms Ramsahai. "I could assign some more to keep you busy until school starts."

Tyler laughed loudly. "No, thanks," he said. "Next you'd

assign me to climbing Mount Everest. Who knows where I'd end up?"

"Now let's all go and cheer for Sam's big finish."

Other books you'll enjoy in the Sports Stories series...

Baseball

❏ *Curve Ball* by John Danakas #1
Tom Poulos is looking forward to a summer of baseball in Toronto until his mother puts him on a plane to Winnipeg.

❏ *Baseball Crazy* by Martyn Godfrey #10
Rob Carter wins an all-expenses-paid chance to be bat boy at the Blue Jays spring training camp in Florida.

❏ *Shark Attack* by Judi Peers #25
The East City Sharks have a good chance of winning the county championship until their arch rivals get a tough new pitcher.

❏ *Hit and Run* by Dawn Hunter and Karen Hunter #35
Glen Thomson is a talented pitcher, but as his ego inflates, team morale plummets. Will he learn from being benched for losing his temper?

❏ *Power Hitter* by C. A. Forsyth #41
Connor's summer was looking like a write-off. That is, until he discovered his secret talent.

❏ *Sayonara, Sharks* by Judi Peers #48
In this sequel to *Shark Attack*, Ben and Kate are excited about the school trip to Japan, but Matt's not sure he wants to go.

Basketball

❏ *Fast Break* by Michael Coldwell #8
Moving from Toronto to small-town Nova Scotia was rough, but when Jeff makes the school basketball team he thinks things are looking up.

❏ *Camp All-Star* by Michael Coldwell #12
In this insider's view of a basketball camp, Jeff Lang encounters some unexpected challenges.

❏ *Nothing but Net* by Michael Coldwell #18
The Cape Breton Grizzly Bears prepare for an out-of-town basketball tournament they're sure to lose.

❏ *Slam Dunk* by Steven Barwin and Gabriel David Tick #23
In this sequel to *Roller Hockey Blues*, Mason Ashbury's basketball team adjusts to the arrival of some new players: girls.

❏ *Courage on the Line* by Cynthia Bates #33
After Amelie changes schools, she must confront difficult former teammates in an extramural match.

❏ *Free Throw* by Jacqueline Guest #34
Matthew Eagletail must adjust to a new school, a new team and a new father along with five pesky sisters.

❏ *Triple Threat* by Jacqueline Guest #38
Matthew's cyber-pal Free Throw comes to visit, and together they face a bully on the court.

❏ *Queen of the Court* by Michele Martin Bossley #40
What happens when the school's fashion queen winds up on the basketball court?

❏ *Shooting Star* by Cynthia Bates #46
Quyen is dealing with a troublesome teammate on her new basketball team, as well as trouble at home. Her parents seem haunted by something that happened in Vietnam.

❏ *Home Court Advantage* by Sandra Diersch #51
Debbie had given up hope of being adopted, until the Lowells came along. Things were looking up, until Debbie is accused of stealing from the team.

❏ *Rebound* by Adrienne Mercer #54
C.J.'s dream in life is to play on the national basketball team. But one day she wakes up in pain and can barely move her joints, much less be a star player.

Ice Hockey

❏ *Two Minutes for Roughing* by Joseph Romain #2
As a new player on a tough Toronto hockey team, Les must fight to fit in.

❏ *Hockey Night in Transcona* by John Danakas #7
Cody Powell gets promoted to the Transcona Sharks' first line, bumping out the coach's son, who's not happy with the change.

❏ *Face Off* by C. A. Forsyth #13
A talented hockey player finds himself competing with his best friend for a spot on a select team.

❏ *Hat Trick* by Jacqueline Guest #20
The only girl on an all-boy hockey team works to earn the captain's respect and her mother's approval.

❏ *Hockey Heroes* by John Danakas #22
A left-winger on the thirteen-year-old Transcona Sharks adjusts to a new best friend and his mom's boyfriend.

❏ *Hockey Heat Wave* by C. A. Forsyth #27
In this sequel to *Face Off*, Zack and Mitch run into trouble when it looks as if only one of them will make the select team at hockey camp.

❏ *Shoot to Score* by Sandra Richmond #31
Playing defense on the B list alongside the coach's mean-spirited son is a tough obstacle for Steven to overcome, but he perseveres and changes his luck.

❏ *Rookie Season* by Jacqueline Guest #42
What happens when a boy wants to join an all-girl hockey team?

❏ *Brothers on Ice* by John Danakas #44
Brothers Dylan and Deke both want to play goal for the same team.

❏ *Rink Rivals* by Jacqueline Guest #49
A move to Calgary finds the Evans twins pitted against each other on the ice, and struggling to help each other out of trouble.

❏ *Power Play* by Michele Martin Bossley #50
An early-season injury causes Zach Thomas to play timidly, and a school bully just makes matters worse. Will a famous hockey player will be able to help Zach sort things out?

❏ *Danger Zone* by Michele Martin Bossley
When Jason accidentally checks a player from behind, the boy is seriously hurt. Jason is devastated when the boy's parents want him suspended from the league.

❏ *Ice Attack* by Beatrice Vandervelde
Alex and Bill used to be an unbeatable combination on the Lakers hockey team. Now that they are enemies, Alex is thinking about quitting.

❏ *Red-Line Blues* by Camilla Reghelini Rivers
Lee's hockey coach is only interested in the hotshots on his team. Ordinary players like him spend their time warming the bench.

❏ *Goon Squad* by Michele Martin Bossley #63
Jason knows he shouldn't play dirty, but the coach of his hockey team is telling him otherwise. This book is the exciting follow-up to *Power Play* and *Danger Zone*.

❏ *Ice Dreams* by Beverly Scudamore #65
Twelve-year-old Maya is a talented figure skater, just as her mother was before she died four years ago. Despite pressure from her family to keep skating, Maya tries to pursue her passion for goaltending.

Roller Hockey

❏ *Roller Hockey Blues* by Steven Barwin and Gabriel David Tick #17
Mason Ashbury faces a summer of boredom until he makes the roller hockey team.

Running

❏ *Fast Finish* by Bill Swan #30
Noah is a promising young runner headed for the provincial finals when he suddenly decides to withdraw from the event.

Sailing

❏ *Sink or Swim* by William Pasnak #5
Dario can barely manage the dog paddle, but thanks to his mother he's spending the summer at a water sports camp.

Soccer

❏ *Lizzie's Soccer Showdown* by John Danakas #3
When Lizzie asks why the boys and girls can't play together, she finds herself the new captain of the soccer team.

Swimming

❏ *Water Fight!* by Michele Martin Bossley #14
Josie's perfect sister is driving her crazy, but when she takes up swimming — Josie's sport — it's too much to take.

❏ *Taking a Dive* by Michele Martin Bossley #19
Josie holds the provincial record for the butterfly, but in this sequel to Water Fight! she can't seem to match her own time and might not go on to the nationals.

❏ *Great Lengths* by Sandra Diersch #26
Fourteen-year-old Jessie decides to find out whether the rumours about a new swimmer at her Vancouver club are true.

❏ *Pool Princess* by Michele Martin Bossley #47
In this sequel to *Breathing Not Required*, Gracie must deal with a bully on the new synchro team in Calgary.

Track and Field

❏ *Mikayla's Victory* by Cynthia Bates #29
Mikayla must compete against her friend if she wants to represent her school at an important track event.

❏ *Walker's Runners* by Robert Rayner #55
Toby Morton hates gym. In fact, he doesn't run for anything — except the classroom door. Then Mr. Walker arrives and persuades Toby to join the running team.

❏ *Mud Run* by Bill Swan #60
No one in the S.T. Lovey Cross-Country Club is running with the pack, until the new coach demonstrates the value of teamwork.

❏ *Off Track* by Bill Swan #62
Twelve-year-old Tyler is stuck in summer school and banned from watching TV and playing computer games. His only diversion is training for a triathlon race … except when it comes to the swimming requirement.